DELINQUENT CHACHA

BY

VED MEHTA

FACE TO FACE
WALKING THE INDIAN STREETS
FLY AND THE FLY-BOTTLE
THE NEW THEOLOGIAN
DELINQUENT CHACHA

VED MEHTA

DELINQUENT CHACHA

HARPER & ROW, PUBLISHERS
New York, Evanston, and London

ALL THE MATERIAL IN THIS BOOK
ORIGINATED IN *The New Yorker*.

TO

JASPER GRIFFIN

▰▰▰▰▰▰▰▰▰▰▰

"The cow is there," said Ansell, lighting a match and holding it out over the carpet. No one spoke. He waited till the end of the match fell off. Then he said again, "She is there, the cow. There, now."

"You have not proved it," said a voice.

"I have proved it to myself."

"I have proved to myself that she isn't," said the voice. "The cow is *not* there." Ansell frowned and lit another match.

"She's there for me," he declared. "I don't care whether she's there for you or not. Whether I'm in Cambridge or Iceland or dead, the cow will be there."

—*The Longest Journey*,
by E. M. FORSTER

"I COULDN'T let you go without a heart-to-heart talk, could I, Mohan?" my uncle asked, eying me closely. He bulged, expanded, under his long golden coat, tight white pajamas, and starched muslin turban—his attire for festive occasions.

"No," I said. I was leaving New Delhi the next day, to work for a degree in literature at Oxford, and we were having a farewell brunch in the upstairs room of our favorite coffeehouse.

"There has been a special, extra-special bond between us ever since you learned to say 'Chacha,' hasn't there?"

"Of course," I said reassuringly. My uncle was without question the greatest failure in the memory of our family. As if he were born with a foreknowledge of the role he was destined to play, he thought up the appellation "Delinquent Chacha" for himself—"*chacha*" means "uncle" in Hindustani—when he was eight years old and his eldest sister had her first child. Throughout his years at British College, Lahore, instead of slaving over books, he chain-smoked and played poker, and he achieved the notoriety of scoring the lowest marks in the college. Though all my other uncles had successfully competed for government jobs and had become important, he worked for his living only once, as a master carpenter, in a shop my father bought him. By the end of the first week, Delinquent Chacha had mortgaged the establishment, lost the money in one hand of Five Card Draw, and started on his long and successful career as a poor relation. His brothers, according to their means, all helped to support him. Some aided him by direct monthly contributions, others by taking him and his wife, Padma, regularly into their houses, still others by adopting one, two, or three of his thirteen children. He farmed out his babies with a benign smile, saying, "Sister, I have great good news—a son. He's yours—the bountiful God has given him to you through my offices." Whenever it became known that his wife was with child once again, his brothers called down curses on his head, for they were certain this time it would be a daughter and they would have to start putting aside money for her dowry. But when the child arrived, it almost always turned out to be a boy, and so great was the relief throughout the family that there was more celebration at the arrival of Delinquent Chacha's children than at the arrival of almost anyone else's. With the passing of each year, he fortified, in legend, his favored place with the gods, acquiring a position all his own among the elders. We children found him incomparable also, for he was the only grownup always at our beck and call. Indeed, he spent most of his time with us; he was a referee at our

2

games, a peacemaker in our squabbles. Later, in our troubled teens, we discovered in our childhood friend an instructor in the harsh ways of the world.

Turning around now, he addressed the boy waiter, who was adjusting an electric fan near a large picture window. "Bearer! Is Delinquent Chacha's special Ceylonese tea ready? See that the cashew nuts are hot, well coated with spices. Today is an extra-special day."

"Yes, Sahib, extra-special day," the boy echoed, rushing to our table.

"And bring fish and chips and a glass of fresh buttermilk, on the *double*, for Kakaji," Delinquent Chacha ordered, pointing to me—he often called me "Youngster." "This is Kakaji's day."

"Yes, General Sahib," the boy said, promoting Delinquent Chacha.

"And don't dawdle. Run like a peacock. And tell the chef that if he allows anyone up here I'll cut his throat. We are having a *very* private meeting."

"Right away, General Sahib, right away." The boy hurried to the head of the stairs and pattered down the steps.

"Wretch," Delinquent Chacha said affectionately. "He lacks the *dignity* of a bearer, but I like spirited boys who have a soul of their own. You don't feel guilty, do you, meeting your Delinquent Chacha this way?"

"No," I said.

In seeing Delinquent Chacha, I was disobeying my

3

father. He did not so much object to my taking leave of my uncle as wish to save me from being exhausted by send-off dinners and coffee and tea parties with each of our hundred relatives. "They can all wave their good-byes at the aerodrome," he had said, warning me not to make exceptions and wound other relatives. When my mother protested "Is it every day a boy from our colony goes away to England?" he brushed this aside with "We can't begin to visit your parents, brothers, sisters, and countless nieces and nephews, and then cart the boy to my side of the family. He has enough on his hands as it is."

My uncle took out his brass condiment case from a stuffed inside pocket and, by rapidly folding tobacco, lime, and black betel-nut parings into a moist leaf, made himself a pan. "Ah, what I wouldn't give to have studied at Ox-Ford," he said, and sighed. "I have never had the heart to tell you, but knowing from the beginning that I could never even see the Ox-Ford spires ruined my life. I have had to make the best of a bust hand, you see. Had an Ox-Ford education been in the ante of my karma, today I would be the rajah of the family. Like your father, I would keep a motorcar, have a membership in the New Delhi Metropolitan Club, give lectures at Government House, and be the secretary of the Racing Club. And I would *never* miss a Sunday of golf. Ever since I was a child, I've had a hankering after golf, you know. Cards were just a substitute." He made me a pan and, handing it over, said, "Do wash your mouth before you go home. I wouldn't like your father to think I am a bad influence." He dipped another leaf in a glass of water and began making a second pan for himself.

"I don't know," he went on gravely, "whether your generation could ever appreciate Ox-Ford. It took the *British* to teach us how to live. Now that they have gone home, there is darkness and anarchy all around us— Muslims, Hindus, Sikhs, Christians are all at each other's throats, and no one is there to arbitrate, to tell us what is right and what is wrong. In the good old twenties, not even the most farsighted pundit had any idea that the British would go, and that in a flash Multan would disappear into a new state of Pakistan and all our family would become refugees in New Delhi, with only the memory of their lost home to support them." He fitted his pan into his mouth, and exhaled a deep breath. "I don't usually go in for black betel nut. It's too expensive. But today is a special day, extra-special day, isn't it? I wanted this meeting," he said, now smiling like his usual self, "to tell you the complete story about S. S. S. Singh. I don't think I've ever told you the *complete* story. What an *ideal* of a man! You know, he was the only man from Multan ever to go to Ox-Ford. I remember so well the day of his coming home—September 3, 1926. When his train pulled into the station, the fathers of all the unmarried damsels were there. Before the returning hero could touch the ground, they lifted him out of the

5

train and carried him on their shoulders. Such was the press of people that his mother couldn't get near him. 'Singh-ingh-ingh, *my* daughter is the prettiest!' they all chanted. Singh kept on saying gallantly, 'Yes, yes,' and each father was certain that the offer of his daughter had been accepted. All Singh was saying, of course—in the chivalrous, British, Ox-Ford manner—was that *all* the Multani damsels were pretty. But, marching along the road to Singh's home, the fathers crooned wedding songs, as though their daughters were already betrothed. You can, however, say this much for the Multanis in the good old twenties"—Delinquent Chacha put on his proudest expression—"they had *standards*. They didn't carry just anyone on their shoulders. I think Singh was the only man to be so honored, and what a good specimen he was of your university!"

As far as Delinquent Chacha was concerned, I was already at Oxford, and there was something about the way he talked that made me feel I actually was. "Just to behold Singh," he continued, transported, "was a pleasure. Early in the morning, he was always to be found in lovely silk knee breeches and an embroidered smoking jacket. By midmorning, he had changed to neat khaki shorts. And, for the afternoon, he casually tied a neckerchief around his neck, with just a hint of a knot at his throat. He never wore the same tennis clothes two days in succession. But the most wonderful thing about him

6

was his evening clothes—worsted suits with subdued
stripes, silk handkerchiefs and matching silk ties. At
home, like any one of us, he might change into pajamas—
he was not above that. And if, over his pajamas, he
wore a dressing gown, it was always unobtrusively excellent—it was of soft, pale Jaeger wool. He was as affable
as his clothes, and, strange though it may seem, no one
was ever jealous of him, because everyone knew that he
deserved his clothes. Did he cheat at cards? *Never.* And
if he ever raised as though he had a royal flush, it was
almost as good as though you had seen his hand. He was
as impressive a gentleman as our British District Magistrate, who treated Singh as an equal, walking along the
street with him in public and inviting him home for
breakfast. In our country, some are *born* well, but, if
Singh is an example, in England birth isn't everything;
they can remake a man completely. They can even
change the color of his skin, for when Singh came back
he was as fair as any Englishman I had ever seen. . . . I
have always felt that the British never wanted to rule us.
They were simply waiting until we were as educated as
they were. Otherwise, how do you explain that Singh,
who before he went to England talked and walked and
looked exactly like me, came back in a sahib's avatar?
I've asked this question of everyone since September 3,
1926, and no one, not even your father, has been able to
give me a satisfactory answer."

7

"Here I am, Hazoor!" the bearer cried, scrambling up the stairs. He held out the big plate of steaming cashews for my uncle to savor.

"Don't you see, wretch, I'm in the middle of my pan?" Delinquent Chacha scolded. The bearer tried to look wilted. But just as he was about to put the plate down on the table, my uncle snapped up a handful of nuts and tasted them. "Chef has done *wonders*," he said, wiping his hands clean of salt and spices. "Don't you tell him, however, or the next time he won't try."

The boy put down the plate of nuts and the pot of tea in front of Delinquent Chacha, and then served my fish and chips, with a glass of buttermilk. He stood aside, waiting for orders.

"Come here," my uncle said to him. "Would you like some nuts?"

"No, thank you, General Sahib."

"Why not?"

"Why not?"

"Yes, why not?"

"Well, General, it's not in my karma. God did not will it so."

"That is a good answer." My uncle laughed, and forced some nuts into the boy's apron pocket. The bearer retired to a corner to eat them, and, putting some sugar and milk in his tea, my uncle resumed, "As the boy said, it's all in the karma. Many of your uncles got straights and better, and they're not as happy as *I* am."

8

He leaned across the table, picked up two of my chips, and, dipping them in tomato sauce, ate them. "They have the *cards*," he continued, "but know nothing of the play."

IS Singh still working in the south, as Chief Minister to the Nizam of Hyderabad?" I asked, half an hour later, as I poured myself a cup of my uncle's tea.

"Kaka, you must put some milk in that tea—it neutralizes the tannic acid," he said hastily.

"Yes. You have never told us why he left our province of Punjab to go away to the foreign south."

"Hmm. What did you say?" Delinquent Chacha's mouth closed tightly over his words—always a sign of displeasure with him.

I repeated my question.

"I have never had the heart to tell any of you children the truth, the tragedy, of Singh before," he said, in a flat, colorless voice. "It all started in Simla. As you know, in those early years I used to go to that hill station myself, with your father—he never missed a summer—and I was detailed to take your eldest sister, Meena, for walks. It was on these outings that I first came to know Singh well. The time of his riding, as our good fortune would

9

have it, always coincided with our walks, and whenever his eyes lighted on us he would dismount from his mare, pat Meena on the head, and say a few chosen words to me. They would set me up for the rest of the day. I don't want to give you the impression that we were the only ones for whom he stopped; he did it for many people, even though he couldn't trot along the Mall Road without everyone, including the rickshaw coolies, greeting and salaaming him. Each season, he rented the Garden Bungalow, at the bottom of the hill, practically next to the Viceroy's summer palace. His cottage was renowned for high-stake, genial poker. I think he would have allowed even a humble person like me to join his celebrated parties if I had had an anna to my name. He was very thoughtful in that way. In the best tradition of English gentleman, he was a man of complete leisure, and I think that even today everyone would acknowledge that under his secretaryship the Blue Room Club flourished as it had never done before—or, for that matter, has done since. . . . For some reason, Singh never competed for the Indian Civil Service, although, of course, no one ever had any doubt that if he did so he would top the list; many of the I.C.S. officers who gave themselves airs didn't have half his intelligence or charm. My own surmise was—and you must remember that I kept up with him very closely—he didn't go in for I.C.S. because he was too good for it; it would have been a waste of a good man. When King Edward's Fund for the Poor was established, Singh presented himself as a candidate for its secretaryship. No one wanted to compete against him, and many who had already submitted their applications quickly withdrew them. After the closing date, it was announced that Singh had only one competitor, a brazen Parsi. He was new to Simla, and probably the only man in the hill station who had never heard of Singh. Many of us tried to tell old Tarporewala that his candidacy was hopeless, but he turned out to be a diabolical man. Nothing would dissuade him. Two days before the selection, he went up before the Public Service Commission and said that he had written to St. Paul's, Singh's Ox-Ford college, to check up on his rival and they had replied that they couldn't find S. S. S. Singh on their books. The Commission brushed him aside, saying that if St. Paul's didn't know about Singh, then he must have been at some other college. Old Tarporewala immediately telegraphed a complaint to the Viceroy, Lord Buxton, here in New Delhi. Back came orders from His Excellency to investigate fully the credentials of the applicants. The date of selection was postponed, and Singh was asked to file his matriculation certificate and honors degree. Singh said he didn't have them. Was Ox-Ford a German spa, from which tourists brought back souvenirs? Who in the world carried a piece of paper from *the* University to show he had been there? The Alma Mater was apparent in the face, clothes, and movements of her graduates. As an alternative to his producing the certificates, the Commission settled upon a cable to his college, but Singh said that he had no one college; he said he was a University man, and hadn't found it necessary to tie himself down firmly to 'a set of snobberies enclosed in a building.' The Commission right away saw his point of view, and cabled the University, but the registrar replied that everyone at Ox-Ford had to belong to a college. None of the Commission members were Ox-Ford–Cambridge men, and they couldn't clear the thing up among themselves. They agreed that there was some confusion somewhere— probably in faraway England. So they called in the District Magistrate, but the D.M. turned out to be a Cambridge man, who doubtless begrudged Ox-Ford its better name. When he was told of the exchange of cables, he said without much emotion, as though he'd never breakfasted with Singh, 'Bother. Singh must be a fake. You can't take the chap seriously. The man probably has never set foot in Ox-Ford.' The position automatically went to the Parsi, whom any Punjabi, had any remained in the competition, could have roundly defeated. Singh resigned from all his clubs and boards, and gave up the Garden Bungalow. His reputation immediately dropped so low that no one now would have dared marry his daughter to him. Soon he was not received at any home except your father's. Such *hypocrisy*. Before the First World War, at the height of the British raj, something like this could never have happened. But even in the twenties the change had set in, and poor Singh had no choice but to run away. He headed straight for the private princely states, hoping that there things might still be what they used to be. In Patiala, he found that word of his disgrace had preceded him, so he made for Kashmir, but there, too, his ill-wishers had done their dirty work. In Nabha, his fate was no better. He moved down south, where no northerner since the beginning of time has ever flourished. When I last heard of him, he was a mere clerk in the service of the Nizam of Hyderabad. To this day I have remained loyal to his glorious memory. I never cease wondering *why* it didn't occur to the authorities that in such a gentlemanly place as Oxford people wouldn't be *bothered* with keeping records. Of course Singh was a University man."

THE bearer returned with the bill. My uncle initialled it absently.

"I suppose I must go," I said. "There is less than twenty-four hours till my departure time."

"Yes, everyone at home must be looking for you. But I haven't told you the main thing I arranged this meeting for," he said, looking through me. "All my life I've been tied down to my mistakes. Now I want to break loose,

13

do something for myself, something that I feel is in my karma, but until now I haven't had the opportunity to bring it about. Do you understand what I mean?"

"You've had a good life," I said. "A very good life."

"No, no, let's not go into all that. . . . You see, all my children are well placed; they are in excellent hands. I think, considering everything, I have done well by them, haven't I? What they do with their lives now is up to them and their karmas."

I nodded.

"I have been reading of late in the newspapers," he went on, "that there is a scarcity of officers to work in England in the post, telegraph, and telephone offices— places like that. The government has been having difficulty in finding English recruits, so they have been taking in naturalized Indians, Pakistanis, Ceylonese. They give them a year or two of education and then straightaway make them officers in the lower rungs of the Civil Service." He pulled out a tattered booklet from his inside coat pocket and put it in front of me. It had no cover, but "Ruskin Delegacy for Adult Education: Oxford" was stamped on the first page. "I have read this many times," he said, tapping the leaflet. "Singh got it for me originally. It says in here that it is never too late to be an undergraduate, and that some of the students connected with the Delegacy are as old as fifty-five, sixty. *I* am only forty-six." He looked at me significantly. His voice dropped to a whisper. "I know you can

keep a secret. For twenty-five years, I have been culti-
vating that tightfisted Multani, Lala Ram Chandar, who
now lives by the Old Delhi wall. I think I can wangle
some money from him."

"But—"

"Don't say a thing," he broke in. "Just take my word
for it. I have with the Lala the equivalent of at least
eighteen hundred and twenty-seven rupees—the exact
fare of a passage to England—in good will. What do
you say to that? All I need is a letter of admission to get
my passport. . . . You are stupefied." He gave a long,
ringing laugh. "Your amazement is nothing to what all
the family will feel when I break the news to them in a
postcard with a Suez stamp. 'My dear elder brother,' I
will write your father. 'As the head of our clan, you are
the person I thought of writing to first. You have been
wondering where I am. No doubt even this minute
police are looking for me all over India. Well, tell them I
got bored in your country and have joined your son as
an undergraduate at Ox-Ford University. Please address
all my post to Delinquent Chacha, Esquire, care of
Ruskin Delegacy for Adult Education, Ox-Ford, England.' Hah! What do you say to that, eh? What do you
think of *that?*"

I felt happy and lightheaded. The idea of having
Delinquent Chacha at Oxford! It was too much. We
talked excitedly together, as though both of us were
already there.

"There are one or two details which you must help me settle," he said. "As soon as you arrive, first thing you must do is to file an application for me at the Delegacy and alert the English government that I am eager and ready to serve them—to devote the rest of my life to their great Civil Service. As soon as my admission goes through, send me the letter by registered post. . . . We must be off. You are not to breathe a word to anyone. Promise? Let's shake on it."

He held my hand in a firm, powerful grip, like an Englishman.

O NE morning, when I picked up my post outside the oak—I'd been living at Oxford for a year now—I was jolted to find a thick letter from Delinquent Chacha. Rubbing my eyes, I looked at the envelope again. The stamp was unmistakably cancelled in Suez, and it could only mean that he was bound for Britain. At the same time, he was midway to realizing his lifelong ambition to pass for a gentleman; he had ineptly added "Esq." to the sender's name, and written out my address with a few too many flourishes. Pulling up an easy chair in front of the fire—it was Saturday, and there were no lectures—

I put my feet on the grate, slit open the bulging envelope, and settled down to read the epistle. It was almost as thick as a small pad, and the pages were still stuck together, as though the writer had intended a book. But the salutation was in English and read from left to right, while much of the text was in Urdu and ran in the other direction. The sheets were so speckled with English phrases and sentences, with sometimes a line changing direction halfway, that just to glance at a page was to have a sensation of seasickness. The style was windy and uncertain throughout:

"My dear, dear Mohan, or may I still address you as Kaka? In the name of St. George, St. Andrew, St. David, and St. Patrick, the bewitching patron saints of our erstwhile rulers, I greet you. My present abode is none other than the Britannia, and what a miracle of comfort and engineering this ship is! In every way it is a floating palace. I'm not exaggerating a bit when I say that on my deck I feel grander than any maharajah, and the vale of Kashmir is nothing to the expanse of ocean stretching at my feet. I may further tell you that the billowing waves prove that the giant I used to tell you stories about is taking a personal interest in your Delinquent Chacha's leisurely progress to England; every time he shakes his stick, we go forward with a song in our hearts. The sensation is no less delirious than walking on an undulating Persian carpet. I waved my handkerchief to Bombay, the downtrodden, doomed city, and to India, on which the sun permanently set the day the British left, only a few hours ago, but I feel I am already in the United Kingdom. Indeed, to be on His Majesty's ship is, in point of law, to enjoy the same privileges and rights extended to Englishmen. For two hundred years, thanks to their graciousness, we enjoyed those rights and privileges, but we flung the gift in their faces because we preferred anarchy and atavism to law and marching with the times. . . . I needn't go on."

It was characteristic of Delinquent Chacha to indulge himself in such rhetoric instead of instantly explaining how an impoverished dreamer had wangled a passage to England. "I know, I know," he went on uncannily, "you want to be told all at once, but it's an involved story and happily it's ten days before we touch our first port; I have plenty of time for composition. To go on, remember the farewell lunch we had a year ago in the Coffee House when you were leaving for hallowed Oxford? Well, you wouldn't recognize the place now. It has expanded into the building next door, and all the walls upstairs and downstairs are draped with red silk and tapestries depicting our world-famous nude sculptures. The boy bearer has departed, and a dozen older men in black livery and red turbans and with manners worthy of footmen of a Duke have taken his place. I need hardly add that the jukebox and the loudspeaker are gone, too; the air is now inhabited by subdued live music of the strings, played by Goanese gentlemen, whose fingers alone can produce good music in our dreary country. From morning to evening, the clientele is edified by Viennese waltzes and sometimes by the beat of the rumba and samba, played always, though, at a slow, genteel tempo. Every time the portals open to receive or let out a customer, some of the music spills out into the street, and this, as you can imagine, has had a great effect on loafers, hawkers, and passersby, who when in the vicinity of the Coffee House—it maintains its old name—walk with a lighter and bouncy step. But alas, Kaka, our favorite place, our old hangout, until yesterweek was no longer within the means of your poor Delinquent Chacha, to whom fate has dealt a very bad hand, even in a country where no one has good hands. But your Delinquent Chacha—as you know all too well—has ever been banking on luck turning, though after you wrote me that the Ruskin Delegacy for Adult Education had no scholarships for Indian nationals my heart did indeed sink; a man at forty-six must start counting his chickens, or else. Faithfully every morning, taking my hope and my walking stick, I set out for my elevenses at the Coffee House. For most of the bitter winter, however, your Delinquent Chacha had no alternative but to wistfully look into the windows, chain-smoke—I spent my Coffee House allowance on king-size cigarettes and special black betel-nut pans—and watch people come and go. I needn't tell you, who know that I am a youngster at heart, how much benefit I received from my pavement watching. A person with less knowledge of the ways of the world, one of those rustics who have taken on the airs of a city man, would no doubt be content eating and belching and talking to women relatives. In time, the clientele, especially the Western, civilized ones, began relying on your Delinquent Chacha; when they were in desperate straits, couldn't make their Indian drivers understand directions and addresses, or were stranded with punctures, Delinquent Chacha was on hand to see them through the fires and waters of Indian travel. One day, an American gentleman, fresh as the morning dew, came out of the Coffee House and marched up to me. He held out his milky-white hand. 'I am Harry Hartwell,' he said. 'I am Delinquent Chacha,' I said, sizing him up. 'In Hollywood we go in for stage names,' he said, 'but I had no idea the fashion had caught on in New Delhi.' I explained to him that 'chacha' means 'uncle' in Hindustani. 'And "delinquent"?' he insisted. I thought that was a little much from a stranger, but gave him a courteous answer. 'You see, Mr. Hartwell, I don't quite fit into the pattern of things here,' I said, 'and "delinquent" is a sort of shorthand for saying I am old-fashioned. To tell the truth, life hasn't done well by me.' 'Hard-luck story, eh?' he said, taking me by the shoulder. 'Your English—isn't too bad.' 'Mr. Hartwell,' I said, 'I come from one of the most educated families in all of Punjab. Two of my brothers are Joint Secretaries in the Ministries, one is a retired major, one is at the moment

the Ambassador to an Arab country, and my nephew'—
you, Kaka—'is at Oxford, in a four-hundred-year-old
college.' 'Well, then, Mr. Delinquent Chacha, why not
come in and join me for a cup of coffee?' Hartwell said.
His calling me Mister warmed my heart. But I couldn't
think of going into the Coffee House in my woollen
pajamas and loose shirt—curse the day that someone
thought up this embarrassing dress for our people—and
being treated condescendingly by the self-important
bearers. I pleaded an urgent engagement at the Ministry
of External Affairs, and made an appointment with him
for the next morning. Next day, I got out my gold long
coat, white pajamas, and muslin turban, which had been
lying in camphor ever since our festive farewell lunch. I
had to walk around the streets for nearly two hours to
shake the smell out of them, but I arrived at the Coffee
House in time to capture a table at our old spot upstairs.
It was there that Mr. Hartwell and I talked, to the sound
of strings. 'So the day was convenient after all,' he said,
sitting down, and, without wasting a second on pleasant-
ries, directly addressed himself to business. 'Now, Delinquent,' he said, 'do you mind if I call you by your
Christian name? You can call me Harry. Can you be
packed and ready to go in two weeks? That's essential.' I
didn't ask any questions, just nodded knowingly. 'I am a
producer, and in three weeks' time we are shooting a real
blockbuster on the Riviera. The story line is a dilly. An
old-fashioned maharajah, who looks like a Buddha and

has acted like a rake, is wintering in Cannes with his entourage, which includes his three hundred or so concubines. He calls them beads, and, Delinquent, you can take it from me that he goes through them like beads. For his lodgings he has taken over an abandoned nunnery. The mother queen—what do you call them in Hindustani?' 'Maharani,' I said. 'The maharani is installed in the rooms of the mother superior, and the other beads, equivalent to the ranks of sisters and novices and such, are likewise quartered in rooms fit for their station. A nunnery is a perfect cosmic stage, and while the drama will be told wholly on the level of sex, its message will be deeply religious. You ought to understand that, because nowhere is there a purer union of religion and sex than here in India.' My spirits soared. To be a maharajah, even if only for the time of the shooting, and be it on celluloid—what ecstasy! And the idea of the beads wrapping themselves around me—be it for the purpose of sets and scenes—oh, Kaka, I cannot put down on paper all the thoughts that tumbled into my mind! As you know, I've always had a little bit of the actor in me, but who, who would have thought that my destiny was to take me by surprise like this? Nevertheless, I was gripped with fear that Hartwell would slip out of my fingers like a myna, who sits in your hand as gentle as a jackdaw and at the first opportunity, a little loosening of the fingers, bites and flies away, only to mock at you from the freedom of the open skies. I put a pan in my mouth and started chewing on it loudly. I asked in a very offhand way, 'Why me?' You, Kaka, can understand such a question at such a time, for, as you know, the only touchstone in my life has been curiosity. Mr. Hartwell replied, 'Look, Delinquent, I know the authentic stuff when I see it, don't I? I've watched you carrying on on the pavement. You see, in Hollywood we work with stars, but in these new countries we have to recruit natural talent.' The strings suddenly went on a softer jag, and the pulse in my temple began beating like thunder. I was afraid Harry would notice it. I redoubled my chewing. Maintaining a nonchalant air, I asked for some details. 'Delinquent, I see you have a good business head,' Harry finally said. I brushed aside the compliment and asked, 'Could you tell me a little more about the picture—the story line, as you call it?' 'Hey, there,' he said, looking at me. 'Does that red stuff you're eating interfere with kissing?' I shook my head. 'It will be good to show it in the maharajah's mouth in the first harem shot,' he said. 'The film will be called "The Rosary," ' he went on, and, Kaka, the next minute Harry had assumed the avatar of that very myna and pecked, oh, *bit* the loving, caressing hand of your Delinquent Chacha. The part he offered me was not that of the maharajah, or one of his Ministers, who by right avail themselves of the concubines lying fallow, or, indeed, that of the chauffeur, whose job it is to scout around the hillsides for wenches, fresh recruits. Oh, Kaka, he offered me the job of a seraglio sweeper, an untouchable from whom every concubine, however aged and ugly, must avert her face and, holding her nose, run away. I told Harry that the job was beneath the dignity of our family rank. I made as though to go. 'Wait a minute, Delinquent,' he said, putting a restraining hand on my arm. 'It's a very good part I'm offering you. The most spectacular sequence concerns the sweeper.' 'But how will I be able to face my people of India, once they have seen me in the guise of a sweeper, and associated with my—' Mr. Hartwell didn't let me finish. 'You see,' he continued, 'the maharajah specially summons an electrical engineer by a letter to President Eisenhower.' I pricked up my ears. 'President General Dwight David Eisenhower?' 'The very man,' Harry said cheerfully. 'The maharajah is quite a rake, and before he takes the way of a Buddha in the closing shots, he writes to Eisenhower asking for the best electrical engineer for an unnamed mission. The President, to avoid precipitating an international crisis, grants the unusual request and flies across a man from the Boeing Company. Then follows a sort of epiphany scene of the rake side of the maharajah; after much wining and dining, and with all the Cabinet members present, the monarch commands the electrical engineer, on pain of death, to build him a bed of rejuvenation. The engineer cunningly stalls, and, just before he escapes with his life to Buenos Aires, eggs on the sweeper to molest the maharajah's current favorite in vengeance for the abortive, perilous mission. The sweeper follows the engineer's instructions to the letter. The whole harem is up in arms. Everyone expects the maharajah to have the sweeper lashed to death, but in a second, contrapuntal epiphany, the spiritual side this time, which follows quick on the heels of the first, the maharajah, in the grandest and most touching scene of all, invokes the name of Gandhi, who fought all his life on behalf of the untouchables—I think he called them "children of God" —and, putting his crown on the sweeper's head, abdicates to follow the path of the Buddha. "The Rosary" ends with an abstract shot of Nirvana, a great, black nothingness and howling, eternal winds.' My spirits soared higher than the sky. The arrangements of my secret departure are too mundane even to bear mention. My only sadness, which is gnawing at me at this writing, is that none of the 'Rosary' stars are travelling on this ship—they are all looking after their own transport, since the picture, because of its experimental nature, is being done on a shoestring. From one point of view, their absence has its advantages; I can practice acting in front of the mirror unhampered, and in the eyes of my cabinmates I am already a meteor to conjure with. . . ."

The letter went on. There were reflections on food, on the sea, on his mates in the ship dormitory. There were admonitions for me, which ended with the remark "But, Kaka, why do I have to advise you on paper? I will soon be with you, and then we can talk things over like old times. I have been a sort of regent to you, giving you advice at every turn of your progress through this incarnation, since you trotted at my side, at the age of four, clutching my forefinger. On my film salary, we will now finance a long, leisurely tour, in a motorcar, of Europe and the Lake District." A little further on, he was confessing that he couldn't summon much enthusiasm for the Riviera. "It's in London and Oxford that I belong; the French are not really gentlemen." And then he was writing about how unhappy and futile his past life seemed from the new vantage point of stardom, and in the closing lines there was a hint—he could never keep anything back—of a little fear he felt: "Oh, Kaka, I worry about the mynas of this world. For how many men have there been on this earth who can understand the springs of a good heart, who are capable of reciprocating affection, and who will not just eat out of your hand as long as it serves their purpose, only to fly away and make a shipwreck of the heart below?"

A MONTH later, I was on an Oxford-to-London train to meet Delinquent Chacha, but I felt anything but happy; his latest communication, incoherent and in places blotched, was as sad as the earlier one had been exultant. The gist of it was that he had lost the stardom to some Indian who had been a professional student in France for many years, and Mr. Hartwell had reneged, if he had ever promised to pay Delinquent Chacha's passage home. Poor as ever, he was now also stranded. "Send money from your scholarship," the letter said. "Meet Delinquent Chacha London 10 P.M. All-India Taj Mahal Curry, Chutney, and Soup Restaurant off Shaftesbury Avenue three days hence." After an unreadable half page: "Will dine." It was signed "Your bleeding uncle."

When I reached the All-India Taj Mahal Curry, Chutney, and Soup Restaurant, I looked through the plate-glass window. There he was, all right. He was clad in his festive long gold coat, and his muslin turban rested beside him on the floor. His back was to the window, and he seemed to be deep in conversation with the only other man in the restaurant. As I entered, a soiled deck of cards materialized from his hand on the table, filling the shabby, empty room with the sound of fluttering birds; it was Delinquent Chacha's famous shuffle. He was so adept at mixing the deck that he never missed a card, and he often used to say, "Would that luck was equally kind to me." He looked around. The deck dropped from his fingers. He was on his feet with his arms around me in a tight hug.

"My long-lost charge," he kept repeating. The stranger, a massive, prosperous-looking man, remained seated at the table, his expressionless, dull face full upon us. "My nephew from Ox-Ford," Delinquent Chacha said, his voice breaking with emotion.

27

"I know," the stranger said, without as much as a nod.

Turning back to me, Delinquent Chacha went on excitedly, "This is the gentleman who has befriended me in England. He is none other than the owner of the All-India Taj Mahal Curry, Chutney, and Soup Restaurant, Lala Suraj Pal himself—from *our* province. He has passed thirty years in England, and, if I may say so, knows everything there is to know about being a gentleman."

Delinquent Chacha seated me next to him and, his knee affectionately touching mine, asked me—between hands of twenty-one with Lala Suraj Pal—about the insides of the Bodleian Library and the Sheldonian Theatre, illustrations of which he had seen in an Oxford guidebook.

"And tell me about Savile Row," he said. "Is the street only a few yards long? You know, it houses more tailors than can be found in all of India. And do the carpets in Harrods really have springs built into them? What, you haven't been there? I'm told it's better than walking on an upholstered couch, and they have miles upon miles of such carpeted corridors. And you've never been to Sotheby's auctions? You've been here all this while and not learned anything about antiques and antiquities? Well, Lala," he said, turning back to the owner, "my Kaka *is* a gentleman, but he's just a little too studious."

The apology fell flat on the Lala's ears; at that moment he was muttering about whether to ask for another card or not. He took one. He made a loud smack and looked as though he were kissing an apparition. It was an ace. "Another," he said hoarsely. He got a two, and a second later he had a five-card twenty-one. The card game went forward, mostly in the Lala's favor. When luck befriended Delinquent Chacha, he shouted to the cook in the kitchen for one more chapatty or a cutlet or a plate of curry, and when luck didn't befriend him, he simply shouted for the same delights to be kept hot and ready. The cook patiently obliged.

"He is the exact replica of the boy bearer we had in the old Coffee House," Delinquent Chacha said to me, "except that he's a little older and more trained." The Lala kept the records of the winnings and losses on a large pad. At the end of the evening, with a loud smack, he announced that he had won two pounds seven and six. For the first time since I came into the room, Delinquent Chacha looked unhappy.

"Lalaji," he said, "I hear that in London"—he pronounced "London" as though the name belonged to his beloved and he had to make up for its ungainliness with his caressing tone—"the times are changing. In the old days, anyone who was at Ox-Ford or had a relation at Ox-Ford, well, his credit was good. A man's word was everything, you know."

It was the turn for the cloud to pass to Lala Suraj Pal's face.

Delinquent Chacha instantly switched his ground.

"Nowadays you can't take anyone's word." He began telling of his misfortune with "The Rosary."

"You told me that before," the Lala said. "In the early part of the evening." Over his shoulder, the Lala acknowledged the cook, standing at attention, and gave him leave to pack up for the night.

"Lalaji," Delinquent Chacha began, again hesitantly, "Kaka has to get back to college tonight, and I was wondering if I could pull a couple of these tables together and catch forty winks here. You know, I have nowhere to go."

The Lala said nothing.

"I could keep watch over the restaurant and make sure—"

"There are no thieves here," the Lala cut in.

"Isn't there any way I could make myself useful?" Delinquent Chacha insisted.

The Lala fell into a deep, Buddhalike silence. Then, coming out of it and being expansive for the first time, he said, "I have been thinking that my restaurant could do with a—mmm . . . porter."

"Yes, yes, porter," Delinquent Chacha said, straightening his collar and putting on his turban.

"There are a hundred Indian restaurants in London," the Lala continued. "Many of them have slipped down into the basement, dimmed their lights, and recruited some you-know-whats to take turns with the clients on the floor and pick their pockets. The All-India Taj

Mahal Curry, Chutney, and Soup Restaurant is one of the few restaurants with their windows respectably above the street, and anyone with a discriminating tongue in his head can testify to my food."

Delinquent Chacha nodded vigorously.

"Business, however, has been none too good," the Lala continued. "None too good. I could do with someone to stand outside on the street invitingly and extoll our virtues. Also, the man could collect the coats, take them upstairs, and bring them down again; at the moment, my customers drop their coats and umbrellas on the banister."

"Oh, Lala! Oh, Lala!" Delinquent Chacha said excitedly. "May God give you a thousand tongues and a thousand liberal hands!"

"Follow me," the Lala ordered, standing up. He lumbered ahead up a dark stairway. On the landing, he unlocked a large broom closet. It was overlaid with cobwebs and crammed with mops and buckets and gallon-size tins of disinfectant and ammonia, and had a musty, choking odor. Delinquent Chacha's spectacles slipped down his nose, and his ever-prompt smile tightened, but it remained a smile.

"You can move out these supplies to the hall cupboard of my flat. I live over there," the Lala said, pointing to a door farther up the stairs. "The business has been bad," he repeated. "All I could offer you is board and room—"

"Kaka, did you hear that? All found in London."

31

"—provided you can fit a bed into this closet—and the baksheesh you collect from the customers."

"Starting tonight?" Delinquent Chacha asked.

"If you like," the Lala said, and he retired to his flat.

I wanted to take Delinquent Chacha with me to the University, but as a scholarship student I had no means of supporting him in Oxford, even for a night. I thought of staying in London with him, but, again, if I did not return to the college that night I risked being gated for the rest of the term.

Delinquent Chacha seated me next to him on the steps and, throwing his leg over mine, said, "Oh, Kaka, who would have thought it? But don't look like that. It won't be so bad. Every diner will spend ten shillings on his dinner, and if there are twenty diners in an evening I should net, say, ten per cent, one shilling a head. One pound. In no time I'll have enough money to pay my twenty-one debt to Lalaji and buy my passage home, and I will be known all over New Delhi as 'England-returned.' I will instruct my grandchildren in the ways of the British, and they will be telling stories to *their* grandchildren about what a grand old gentleman their great-great-grandfather was. And there are worse ways of turning a penny than being a porter. I tell you, some of the most prosperous owners of the biggest restaurants take the coats and hats of their customers, so as to be better acquainted with the clientele, be on good personal terms with them, you know. Tell me, where is there a job in all the world where I needn't get up till lunch-time? Oh, Kaka, I shall be a man of leisure, and I will have all the time in the world to sightsee. In India, when do I get any time? Today your Delinquent Chacha must call on Sheila, because she's having her baby. Tomorrow he must visit his big brother, in order to keep in touch with the family affairs. Every day somebody is being born or getting married or dying, and, however remote our relationship, your Delinquent Chacha, unless he wishes to cut his nose in the family, has to put in an appearance. When does your Delinquent Chacha ever get a moment to edify his mind? Extending hospitality in the All-India Taj Mahal Curry, Chutney, and Soup Restaurant is a perfect—Kaka, I tell you, a perfect—opportunity. It's infinitely better than 'The Rosary.' Why, there I wouldn't have had any time at all, and I couldn't have shown my face in India. Every rustic would have pointed to me and said condescendingly, 'There goes the cinematic sweeper.' Here I will be anonymous, and enjoy a great measure of dignity and self-respect. Don't you see, when Lalaji goes away to Brighton for a weekend or to the Lake District for a rest cure, who will look after his interests, be in charge of the restaurant, be the host, if not me? Oh, Ram, I thank you a million times for my good fortune. Kaka, you must be off. You mustn't let your doting Delinquent Chacha waste your time. Books must come first." He smothered all my entreaties and expressions with tight hugs. "Off

33

with you, off with you," he said, propelling me toward the door. At the bottom landing, he pulled out of his bulging pocket the brass pan case that was as familiar to me as his face. "Kaka, this is the last Indian pan I have. I don't know how long I've been saving it for you." He forced me to take it, and, even before I had wedged it into my mouth, he had gathered my duffel coat from the banister and held it out.

"Oh, no, no!" I cried.

"Delinquent Chacha must get into training," he said cheerfully. "Must get into training. You mustn't disobey your Delinquent Chacha on his first night in London."

I held out my left arm.

"Oh, Kaka, *both* arms!" he said with deep disappointment. "A gentleman holds out both his arms evenly."

With some groping, I found the sleeve holes. Instantly, Delinquent Chacha had slipped the coat on me, and, holding the collar with one hand and reaching from the bottom for my jacket with the other, he pulled my inner coat with an experienced touch. Afterward, making a brush of his hand, he dusted my back and then my front and then my shoulders vigorously, and held open the door.

"Off with you, Kaka," he said.

I went out, and he followed me into the cold. Under the street lamp, he said, "One last word. I don't have to tell you, Kaka, that my ambition has always been to attend Ox-Ford, so when you come to see me here don't bring any of your undergraduate friends along. Some of them might still be there when I enroll in the University, and I wouldn't want them to feel awkward and embarrassed. . . . You know what I mean?" He lowered his voice. "And if I should happen to meet you with one of them on the street, oh, Kaka, don't recognize me!" He threw his arms around me for the final time, and then ran into the restaurant and bolted the door behind him.

I walked around the block, worrying about him, and when I arrived again at the window of the restaurant, I peered in. Delinquent Chacha, stretched out on a couple of tables, with his festive gold coat for a pillow, was fast asleep.

A FORTNIGHT after Delinquent Chacha had landed his job at the All-India Taj Mahal Curry, Chutney, and Soup Restaurant, I came up to London to spend my Christmas holidays, and, following his postcard's instructions, took a tube from Paddington Station to Piccadilly Circus and walked two blocks to the Royal Colonial Club of the British Empire, which Delinquent Chacha had found to be, as he wrote, "a club after my own heart." The club was funereal and dark, and the walls were draped with oversize canvases of departed governors and viceroys, and all manner of regimental ties in display cases lent an additional touch of grandeur.

The porter behind the lobby desk stopped me. "You are the scholar from Oxford looking for Mr. Delinquent Chacha?" he said uncannily. "You are certain to find him, sir, in the Lord Curzon Hall, which is at the end of the passageway at the top of the staircase."

The capacious chairs in the rooms upstairs were occupied almost entirely by ex-colonials. The Lord Curzon Hall turned out to be a long, narrow room, the walls of which were covered with horses, of all sizes and colors, in ornate gilded frames. Delinquent Chacha was seated on an ottoman at the farthest end of the room, opposite a nervous African, who was reading a copy of the *Times*. I rushed up to Delinquent Chacha with outstretched arms, but he didn't respond. I stared at him. Instead of his long gold coat and muslin turban he had on a chalk-striped dark-blue suit with a waistcoat. A price tag reading " £8 10s." hung from his sleeve, giving him the appearance of a human mannequin. Indeed, he looked straight through me, as though I were just another window-shopper.

"Delinquent Chacha!" I cried out, tearing off the tag.

"Sh-h-h," he said, and indicated an easy chair nearby.

"Is anything the matter?" I asked in a whisper, taking the seat.

He put a finger to his lips and shook his head. For some time, Delinquent Chacha, the African, and I sat in a tomblike silence. Finally, Delinquent Chacha shattered it by addressing the African in a clear, booming voice. "My dear sir, a very, very good evening to you!" he shouted.

The African started from his seat.

"My dear, dear sir," Delinquent Chacha went on in his friendliest manner. "Are you, perhaps, a long-standing member of our hallowed Royal Colonial Club of the British Empire? I have the greatest desire to belong to it, to be tucked permanently into its fold. As it is, I am here only by the courtesy of a great princely figure whose name I used with aplomb to acquire temporary guest privileges. The good porter downstairs tells me I need two sponsors, one an older member, the other any member in good standing. My business often brings me to London, you know, and it's rather nice, sir, to have, so to speak, as splendid a peg, so to speak, as the Royal Colonial Club of the British Empire to hang my hat on. I only hope, my dear sir, you will not think me too bold for addressing you in this man-to-man manner, but we are sitting in the same club, and it's only appropriate that before you acquiesce to my request you should be made acquainted with my qualifications. I come from one of the best families in India, and my hobby since boyhood has been rearing cub lions and tigers and baby elephants"— Delinquent Chacha had never set eyes on a jungle animal except in the zoo—"and the half year I spend in India I pass in long shikars. They rather bore me, you

37

know, but I am besieged by new ambassadors and American dignitaries, and, *entre nous*, I don't like to—how shall I say—disappoint them; they may take away a bad impression of my country."

The *Times* slipped from the African's hands to the floor, and he stared at Delinquent Chacha. "I thank you from the bottom of my heart," he said. "I thank you for calling me 'sir.' I myself am a temporary member and am scouting for a second sponsor." He darted out of the room.

"Ah, Mohan, Africans have a long way to go," Delinquent Chacha said with a sigh. "A very long way. Frankly, Kaka, I'm not sure they'll ever catch up with us Indians. You see, they have not had the advantage of a chivalrous association with the British." He got up from the ottoman, and came over and sat down on the arm of my chair. He patted me on the back. "You played your silent role beautifully," he said. "Well done, Kaka. Do you like my new suit? I picked it up at Knighted Tailors—by the Queen's appointment, you know. You've seen their advertisements in the Underground stations. I feel free in this British suit. Our long coats are really very constraining to the motion of the legs. And, you know, these Britishers have solved the problem of matching the top and the bottom miraculously. They use the same cloth, but divide it in two. And, Kaka, you know about our pajama cord. It leaves marks around the waist, and your Delinquent Chacha has found breathing

God's good air difficult because of the constriction of his diaphragm. I tell you, the man who invented the trouser belt was a genius on a scale no smaller than the English gentleman who invented the wheel—I forget that gentleman's name for the moment. Ah, yes, your father has worn a suit, and you've worn a suit. But"—he sighed—"your poor Delinquent Chacha has had to be content with a winding sheet. To say the truth, I don't ever again want to have a piece of Indian cloth on my back. It brings bad luck."

"You must be raking in a lot of money as porter at the restaurant," I said.

"No, Kaka," he said. "I just sold all my Indian clothes to a foolish antique dealer who specializes in imperial dress. But I am on the way to becoming the owner of the All-India Taj Mahal Curry, Chutney, and Soup Restaurant one day."

"What?"

"Yes," he said. "Fate is turning. Last night, the owner of our great All-India Taj Mahal Curry, Chutney, and Soup Restaurant, Lala Suraj Pal, fell down the entire length of the stairwell and cracked his coccyx. This is not a part of the anatomy I am familiar with, but the chef tells me it is in the shape of a hook, from which our tail hung in the olden, pastoral days. The effect of it all is that your Delinquent Chacha is, at least for a few days, the proud manager of a restaurant in London, to do with it as he wishes. The business is already showing signs of

39

prosperity." He pulled up a chair next to me, and, putting his feet up on an end table, said sadly, "Oh, Kaka, I look at all these pictures around me and I know immediately that my life has been a failure. I wish I knew the name of every horse here, and who it belonged to. Now, that African gentleman who was sitting here, he probably doesn't care to know such things. I do, and now that we are sitting under the umbrella of the British raj I can tell you that my life somehow got onto the wrong foot when I was sixteen or seventeen, but *not* for the reasons that are usually given among our relatives: Delinquent Chacha never studied; he was always a practical joker; he was misled by bad friends; he never had the benefit of the wisdom of his father, dying as he did before Delinquent Chacha matriculated; he learned to smoke too early. No, Kaka, none of those reasons are wholly true."

"You've enjoyed your life more than anyone," I said. On the rare occasions when he became gloomy, such remarks usually cheered him up, probably because their truth was undeniable.

He cut me short. "I'm a successful gentleman in London now. I don't have to go on beating around the bush anymore, do I?" His voice broke. "Oh, Kaka, in these two weeks in London, what has your Delinquent Chacha not gone through? Here his dream has been realized, and—"

He stopped. A rather beefy man with a long English

face and tousled hair walked into the room. He went over to the chair that had held the African, sat down, picked up the copy of the *Times* from the floor, and, after many matches and puffs, lit his pipe. Delinquent Chacha watched him closely.

Suddenly Delinquent Chacha leaped out of his chair and rushed across the room and began intently examining the canvas of a horse overhead. "Oh, Dobbin," he said wistfully, "if you were running today at Ascot, I would weigh you in gold as the believers do the Aga Khan and back you with the last ounce of it." The Englishman puffed at his pipe. He seemed to be completely absorbed in the *Times,* and looked up only to put another match to his pipe. Undaunted, Delinquent Chacha said, "Kaka, as an Ox-Ford man, and knowing the ins and outs of Newmarket, you ought to be able to appreciate these forelegs." Delinquent Chacha returned to his chair, and said to me in a whisper, "Apparently he doesn't understand gentlemanly overtures." Then, while the Englishman sat with his face buried in the *Times,* Delinquent Chacha continued to address me in his best public voice. Usually, in talking to me, he used a medley of Urdu and English, but now he spoke English exclusively, even when he had to pause in the middle of a sentence to search for appropriate English words for a ready Urdu phrase. "As I was saying, Kaka, in India you will find as many reasons for my not having my feet on the ground at forty-seven as we have relatives, but you and I know

41

better, don't we? Any objective man who knows the Queen and me will tell you I would have appeared on the Queen's honors list by this time as the Companion of the Order of St. Michael and St. George but for one circumstance—my marriage to your auntie. As C.M.G., I would have gone out into the world with the blessings of a patron saint—you know, George is renowned in East and West, among Christians and Mohammedans, as the dragon slayer on horseback—and with a helpful pat on the back from the Archangel Michael himself, the vanquisher of the Devil. I would then never have had to give a thought to being a *successful man*."

I started to say something, but he waved me into silence.

"You see, Kaka, when I was seventeen and in the last year of college, all the women of the house began looking for a good match for me. Ordinarily, my parents would have waited till I was twenty-five, but I was a fiery pony and they wanted to harness me as soon as they could." His voice dropped to a whisper. "Do you think that Brussels sprout of an Englishman is taking all this in?" I said I was sure not. Clearing his throat, Delinquent Chacha went on in his public voice, "The women relatives asked me about what to look for in a wife. I laid down three specifications. I said that she must have a fair skin, not a shade darker than the snow capping our Himalayas—those were my very words—for, among other things, under no circumstances did I

42

wish to be landed with one of our Dravidian girls from South India, you know. Kaka, I have no racial prejudices to speak of, but it is no secret that Westerners prefer the fairer complexion, the straight nose, and the clear-cut features of us northerners to our thick-lipped, snub-nosed, kinky-haired southern brethren—not to mention their charred coloring. I said the second quality was that my wife must play the violin, or at least sing. Music adds a subtle touch and grace to a woman, like the perpetual wearing of a French scent. Also, your Delinquent Chacha wanted an entertainer on call at parties and grand public affairs." He lowered his voice and asked again if I thought the Englishman was taking it all in. I said it was impossible to tell. "But the story is intrinsically interesting, isn't it?" he whispered. I said it was. He resumed with redoubled energy, "Finally, I insisted that my wife must speak English fluently and with a good accent. Kaka, I knew from the very start I was destined for the company of Englishmen, and I wanted a wife who would feel on an equal footing with them. About dowry, sewing and knitting, and supervising the servants in the polishing of brass and silver and such, I didn't give a hang. You see, Kaka, I was a progressive in my own day, just as I am in the avant-garde movement today when I ask for the return to India of the beneficent rule of the British. After turning our province of Punjab upside down, they found a bride who met all my specifications. She was twelve, five years younger than I.

43

A separation of eight or ten years between a husband and wife was considered desirable, but since I was a sort of child prodigy in these matters, not much thought was given to the small difference of years between me and my betrothed. By that time, two of my brothers—your dear uncles, Kaka—had come into the Indian Civil Service, and everyone knew that the younger brothers of I.C.S. officers were looked after. Sight unseen, her father accepted me as his son-in-law-to-be. Kaka, you can tell how far things had gone by the fact that my father-in-law-to-be journeyed two hundred miles from Lahore to our home in Multan with the customary hundred and one rupees to give my mother personally as an acceptance of the bond. I was completely in the dark about his arrival, and that morning a practical joker from the colony challenged me to a wrestling match. To my undying shame, I accepted it. On the whole, I was a studious boy, and as far as I was concerned wrestling was purely for the hooligans. But I changed into a loin strap, and with that as my entire dress I went out into the gully. Within a second, the joker put the illegal double nelson on me, and pinned me to the street. For twenty minutes I struggled to free myself, but he had powerful arms and hands, and the muscles at the back of my neck were as yet tender. When the joker finally let me go, I found a pair of kindly eyes looking at me. They belonged to a very distinguished-looking gentleman who was wearing a gray felt hat and sporting a long ivory cane with a beautiful knob at the top. 'Is young Master about?' he asked. 'You are speaking to him,' I said, getting up off the ground. 'You can't be a reliable servant if you take such liberties with your master's name,' the gentleman with the ivory cane said. 'You see, he is to be my son-in-law, and I am here with a hundred and one rupees to seal the engagement.' How many times in my life since have I not regretted that I didn't rush inside, change into a dapper suit of clothes, and appear in front of him in a new, irresistible avatar! But, oh, Kaka, like a fool, I said, 'Father, I am the very Delinquent Chacha you are looking for.' And, forgetting my sweaty body, I threw myself into my father-in-law-to-be's arms. He shrank back and, turning on his heel, went away, never to be seen again. He took with him the first and the brightest promise of my life; from that time, for me, it has been a run on a downhill slope. I took to my bed. I felt somebody very close to me, somebody I had loved forever, had died, leaving me bereft for the rest of my life. That spring, I naturally failed my B.A. examination. My mother became deeply disturbed about the marital prospects of a failed B.A. Some of the more aggressive women of the house prevailed upon her to advertise in the newspaper. I was taken to the best photographer in Lahore for a studio portrait, and for nearly a fortnight I looked out of the marriage page of the *Tribune*. Oh, Kaka, the picture was so handsome that I hardly recognized myself. It showed me with a rose in my buttonhole. But the caption was even more tempting. It read, in italics, 'Failed B.A. from British College, Lahore. Good University man with two brothers in I.C.S.' To most fathers of daughters it was a dinner plate of banana ice cream on a hot day. Shoals of them began arriving, on bicycles, on foot, on horseback, in tongas, with proposals of their daughter's hand and bigger and bigger dowries, all designed to put a halter on a prize horse. I firmly held out for the three original qualifications. But there was one father more cunning than I. He was a suave District Magistrate, one of the first Indians to hold such an exalted post in the British Empire. He told my mother in no uncertain terms that his daughter met my three specifications entirely. No one had the courage to ask to *see* his daughter; it would have been casting doubt on the District Magistrate's word. If the British could entrust the ruling of the country to him, who were we? In sentiment we were correct, but he was a born defrauder—of governments and Delinquent Chachas. Innocent that I was, I bathed in the luxurious waters of a newborn. The wedding was spectacular—Delinquent Chacha seated on a trim stallion, both covered with shimmering ornaments, bells, and objets d'art, or whatever you call them, and a fierce sword dangling at the equestrian hero's side. In line with the time-honored tradition, Delinquent Chacha chivalrously set forth to the sound of an epithalamic band to take his spouse heroically from the clutches of her parents. Kaka, imagine, if you are able to, poor Delinquent Chacha's disappointment, the heartbreak, when on the nuptial bed, lifting the veil, he discovered underneath a dark and brooding face. She turned out to be a shrew. She couldn't speak a word of English, and her sandpaper voice could not shake out one musical note. My star passed into eclipse, and without the sunny marriage Delinquent Chacha had hoped for he withered away in a day, like the flower in his buttonhole. Divorce there could be no question of; it hadn't been heard of in India for thousands of years, and Delinquent Chacha, in spite of all his progressivism, could not break such iron shackles of the past. He found what comfort there was in bringing forth large and fair progeny, and taking delight in all their achievements. And in this respect, I may say, your father and at least one of your dear uncles have not done badly by my children. I wish I could say that about every one of your good uncles, Kaka." Delinquent Chacha stood up and walked to the center of the room.

"Good sir, a very, very good evening to you," he said.

The Englishman put down his paper, and held another match to his pipe. It was a little time before he answered. "Good evening," he said genially, and looked out of the window.

"This is my nephew—Kaka," Delinquent Chacha said, introducing me. "Would you like to know my name?"

47

"If you like," the Englishman said.

"Delinquent Chacha," Delinquent Chacha said, and he waited for a reaction.

The Englishman looked at his watch. "I think I can just make the showing of that farce around the corner," he said, standing up. He folded his copy of the *Times* neatly and put it on the chair.

"A moment," Delinquent Chacha said agitatedly. "Before you go, what did you think of the sad story of my life?"

"I'm afraid I didn't really listen. That is to say, I couldn't help hearing bits and pieces, but I'm sure I couldn't repeat a sentence of it. I thought you were having a private conversation. Should I have listened?"

"Oh, no, no," Delinquent Chacha said. "As you say, it was a private conversation."

There was a little awkward silence.

"Well," the Englishman said finally, looking at his watch, "I must be off. I'm sure we'll meet again, perhaps here at the club."

"Here at the club," Delinquent Chacha said quietly, his mouth closing tightly in displeasure.

No sooner was the Englishman out of the room than his spirits revived. "Shall we go down and make friends with the porter? It's nice to keep fellows like that on your side."

We walked downstairs, and in the lobby Delinquent Chacha smoked a cigarette with the porter. As we were leaving the club, we passed a large open ledger on a stand, with a notice: "All visitors are requested to write their names and addresses in the visitors' book." Taking the pen from the holder, Delinquent Chacha wrote out in a large hand, "Delinquent-Chacha of the All-India Taj Mahal Curry, Chutney, and Soup Restaurant, the celebrated Indian restaurant off Shaftesbury Avenue, London, United Kingdom." Then he made an extra-long hyphen and appended "C.M.G." to "Delinquent-Chacha." "I should have pumped our good English friend about the proper size of a hyphen," he said, and returned the pen to the holder. "These English things have mysterious nuances."

THOUGH Delinquent Chacha never spoke of the hardships of his job as porter in the All-India Taj Mahal Curry, Chutney, and Soup Restaurant, there was something sad about his standing in the cold, coughing surreptitiously behind his sleeve and opening taxi doors with exaggerated zeal. In India, he had spent more than half his life sitting in comfortable coffeehouses or clubs, lording it over waiters and bearers. We children felt more exalted in his company than in that of our parents.

What he lacked in the way of a successful career he more than made up for with the dignity of his bearing. To walk along beside him was like being in the train of a nawab; from every direction he was greeted with salaams.

I spent my Christmas vac. doing some reading in the British Museum, and whenever I dropped by the restaurant—I made it a point to go there at least once a day, usually after museum hours—I would find him holding forth to strangers, telling them his entire life history: the poker parties of his college days, the horrors of Indian life as he had witnessed them from the streets of New Delhi, the indulgent Hindu family system that allowed a carefree man of leisure like him to produce children to his heart's content and leave to his relatives the responsibility of bringing them up. When I approached him, he wouldn't take any notice of me until he had finished his sentence; then he would turn and pump my hand vigorously, and say, "Oh, my dear nephew, we meet again. Can it be? Tell me instantly all the wisdom you have culled from those great tomes in our hallowed museum." But no sooner would I start to answer than a taxi would draw up and Delinquent Chacha would rush to open the door. He would sadly watch the passengers disappear into a cinema that was next door to the restaurant. Immediately forgetting his disappointment, he would begin to extoll the joys of being in London. "Oh, Kaka, the climate here is as bracing as ours is torpid. Here the streets are beautifully clean; ours are dusty and thickly overlaid with living corpses. By escaping to London, your Delinquent Chacha has added at least twenty-five years to his present, wonderful avatar."

All evening, he was either opening or closing doors. Whoever stopped to talk to him received an earful of questions. How was his health? What was the city of his birth? What was the nature of his profession? Did he have a big family? When the stranger left, Delinquent Chacha leaned negligently against the wall or the lamp-post, with a Players No. 3 prominently displayed between two fingers.

As at home, he was full of schemes for improving his situation. "Kaka, I have been thinking that I should open my own Indian restaurant—nearby, perhaps, or somewhere around Soho Square," he said one day. "I am told that good Victorian houses are going cheap there. Standing here, I have met so many Englishmen who want to keep up their association with us through the medium of good curry. They are just waiting for someone to provide them with a real, old-fashioned India here in the center of London." He left me to open the door of a taxi. In a minute he was back again. "In my restaurant," he continued, as if he had never quit my side, "I could place large blocks of chalk and cork to give the impression of one of our Marabar caves. The English find our caves very romantic and native. You, Kaka, could help me spread the word among the scholars in the British Museum. What do you think of my printing the bill of fare with deckled edges and with a gold-and-silver border, Indian-historical style? They would serve as good bookmarks, and every time a scholar looks up from his book and sees my menu his mouth will water. Or perhaps," he said, shifting his weight to his other foot, "a man such as I has more to offer the English by acquainting them with the total Indian past—of which curry, of course, is only a part. What would you think of importing all our young lady relatives to Britain to illustrate in pantomime the history of Indian womanhood from ancient times to the present? Ah, but one needs a little money for that, and perhaps I ought to let my mind dwell on something that can come true more quickly, by itself."

ONE evening as I approached the All-India Taj Mahal Curry, Chutney, and Soup Restaurant, I saw that Delinquent Chacha was not in his usual place. Without his smiling face at the door, the restaurant seemed closed, and it was in fact empty, except for the cook, who was turning a chapatty on the griddle in the kitchen.

"Where is he?" I asked.

The cook pointed vaguely to the stairway. I ran up to Delinquent Chacha's room and rapped on the unpainted door. I pushed it open when there was no answer. Delinquent Chacha, clad in a pair of drawers and a vest, was seated on the unmade bed with his eyes shut, chanting the name of God. There was a burned-out joss stick and many cigarette butts on the washstand—the only other piece of furniture in the room—and a battered suitcase was open on the floor, with his few clothes flung across it. The weak, unshaded bulb suspended from a chain overhead threw dark shadows on the flanking walls and on the cobwebbed ceiling.

"Delinquent Chacha!" I cried.

"Ram, Ram, Ram," he answered distantly, as though he were a medium.

With his eyes still shut, he drew a square envelope from under his pillow and handed it to me. The envelope was engraved with a coat of arms and addressed to "Delinquent Chacha, C.M.G."

"Dear Sir," the letter began. "I am taking the liberty of writing to you on the suggestion of one Mr. Duganda of Nigeria and the Overseas Lecture Bureau, whose acquaintance I believe you made at the Royal Colonial Club of the British Empire. Because of the influx of new members to our ever-growing world community, the Commonwealth Polytechnical College at Oxford, in conjunction with the Cowley Secretarial Bureau and the

53

Parktown Crammer for Young Ladies, is sponsoring a Model United Nations at Oxford during the first weekend in the Hilary term. In a spirit of generosity, the Oxford City Theatre has offered its capacious facilities to the M.U.N. The topic is: Would this house rather prosper in peace or perish in political pestilence? We have already started electing student delegations to represent the assigned countries." The letter went on to give the days and hours of the meetings of the General Assembly, Eco-Soc, and the fourth and fifth committees, and concluded with a paragraph that Delinquent Chacha had underlined in red ink: "We should be honored if you, sir, would accept our invitation to be one of the four guest speakers from the world at large at the opening session. Lord Whitenorth of Great Britain, Chief Lulu of the Gold Coast, and M. Pobedeniski of Outer Mongolia have all accepted. We regret that, because of the limited time, we are unable to invite speakers from all the worthy and deserving countries onto our platform, but the student delegations will have ample time to air their views from the floor of the house. Believe me, yours faithfully . . ." I looked up. Delinquent Chacha's eyes were now open and glistening.

Many of my young cousins in India had no more use for the British raj than did the native politicians now feasting on the fruits of power. But then, as Delinquent Chacha never failed to remind us, we had been born and brought up in a time of bloodshed and chaos, in a time when millions of people had been set adrift from their ancient homeland because of some such abstract and backward-looking political principle as the one that led to the shameful division of our country and the creation of the quasi-theocratic state of Pakistan. Under the umbrella of the raj, people were left free to practice any religion they wished, without having to demand a state and an army. Nor could we look back, as Delinquent Chacha could, to a time so unlike ours that it was free of corruption, meanness, and petty politicians—politicians who knew more about shopkeeping than affairs of state. To a country for hundreds of years in the throes of factional and sectarian wars, the British had given, for hundreds of years, calmness, justice, and equality. But, alas, at any one time, only a few thousand Britons could be spared to serve in India, and they had kept so aloof that the great majority of our people had not even noticed their innate superiority. Delinquent Chacha was one of the few who had. And how often he had talked about Oxford.

"But what more could you ask? How marvellous!" I exclaimed now. "Maybe it will mean—"

"Oh, Kaka, Kaka," he said. "Don't go on. Don't agitate this fragile heart to the breaking point." He rubbed his left side dramatically. "How your Delinquent Chacha wishes today that he were in India! Oh, would that the Thames were our holy, sacred Ganges, so that with a dip I could quickly become my old sinless self again. Ram, Ram, Ram. That little piece of paper in your fist has aged me more than all the dust and living corpses of our Indian streets—and I was just beginning to take to the exhilarating British climate." I tried to break in, but he went on. "By my signing my name 'Delinquent Chacha, C.M.G.,' Ram, Ram, Ram, in sundry visitors' books—in embassies, places of historical interest, and such—I have created a national scandal, an international incident. I have betrayed my newly found motherland and perhaps jeopardized forever the chances of the British raj's returning and putting an end to our internecine bickerings and wars. How easy were those elegant squiggles of the pen!"

"But how do you know the visitors' books had anything to do with the invitation?"

His head dropped to his chest. "How do I know?" he asked under his breath. "How do I know?" he said, raising his chin. "Oh, Kaka, I don't think I *do* know. I *don't* know. Do you suppose," he went on slowly, "that the Companion of the Order of St. Michael and St. George has been conferred on me and I haven't heard about it? I haven't read the papers lately, it is true. Do you know *when* the Queen mounts her throne and singles out her loyal servants for eternal baksheesh?"

I said that I thought it was sometime around her birthday, and that perhaps it was even called the Birthday List, but he had already lost interest in his own question. He had me in a tight hug and was profusely thanking Ram for setting his mind at ease. "In what unsuspected ways do you, Ram, O my Ram, find a means to enlighten your Delinquent Chacha." He became reflective. "You see, Kaka, from my cursory perusal of the lessons of history, it seems to me that two qualities built the British Empire and kept it sunny side up with its best foot forward—carefully framed legislation, and show of authority. Of the two, authority is much the more important. Without it, legislation is impotent. There can be no authority unless there is a small clique of ruling men who function in the field as disinterested agents of the Queen. That's precisely why I attach such supernatural importance to my title, to titles generally. . . ."

Five minutes later, he was worrying about his "début" at Oxford. "How can I go there in *these* rags? At least thirty sterling guineas are needed for a gown, a mortarboard with a long plaitlike tassel, and a pair of long, romantic boots."

Delinquent Chacha put on his only suit, the dark-blue one with the chalk stripe, and smoothed his black, unruly hair, using the palms of his hands as a pair of military brushes. He washed his face and, when he couldn't find a towel, jerked his head from side to side. When he was satisfied that he looked presentable, we went downstairs. Opening the front door, he leaned against it and lit a cigarette. He thoughtfully massaged his ear. To break the chill of the cold wind, he had developed a habit of alternately rubbing his ears and warming his hands over imaginary chestnuts. The tic, which would have been nerve-racking in anyone else, was almost decorative in him, for he raised his hands to his ears as though he were saluting someone in the distance.

Suddenly he fitted his thumb and forefinger between his front teeth and let out a loud whistle for a taxi, to oblige a couple coming out of the Aristophanes, a lavish two-story Greek restaurant around the corner in a dead-end street. A lady dropped her purse, spilling its contents, and in a matter of seconds Delinquent Chacha was at her side. Both the couple and the woman tried to tip the most accommodating man on the London streets, but he refused grandly, because they were not customers of the All-India Taj Mahal Curry, Chutney, and Soup Restaurant. It habitués—mostly students or small businessmen from India—arrived on foot and left without as much as a sixpence for him.

A schoolboy stopped to study the bill of fare in the window of the Taj Mahal. He was fitted out in a blue-and-purple uniform. Delinquent Chacha studied him carefully, and then, to my surprise, he stepped forward and seized the peak of the boy's school cap. "My good man," Delinquent Chacha said, "it so happens that I am looking for a replica of the suit of clothes you are now wearing."

The schoolboy, freeing his cap, stared at him. Delinquent Chacha turned to me. "Don't you think the cut of this coat can only have issued from a sculptor's hand?" Turning back to the boy, he said, "I will not detain you a minute longer from your urgent and pressing lessons. But it so happens that I am looking for a replica of your suit of clothes for myself; I'm soon going up to the University, and I would be glad if you disclosed the names and addresses of the several tailors who contrived to make this most dazzling adornment for your skin."

"All school uniforms of St. Luke's School in Kensington are made by the School and University Outfitters at the top of Regent Street," the boy said gravely.

"Thank you, thank you!" Delinquent Chacha said. "The School and University Outfitters. You have done your newly discovered Indian friend a great and inestimable service." He let out a loud whistle. The boy jumped. A taxi screeched to a stop, and Delinquent Chacha bundled the bewildered boy into it. "May God speed you to your lessons. You can always find me at the All-India Taj Mahal Curry, Chutney, and Soup Restaurant," he said, and then, to the driver, handing him his last two shillings, "The St. Luke's School in Kensington."

T HE next morning, at the hour that we had agreed
on, I arrived at the tailor's. Delinquent Chacha was
already there. He had the only salesman on the floor—a
man with a smooth, correct smile and a shiny bald head—
by the sleeve. "Oh, Kaka!" Delinquent Chacha shouted
across to me as I entered the shop. "Have you ever seen
in all your life such a delicious queue of bolts of cloth,
begging for attention, like a thousand and one Arabian
tailors? Mr. Stubbs, my nephew from Ox-Ford." Delinquent Chacha introduced me proudly to the salesman.
"Kaka, I have shown Mr. Stubbs the invitation and he
understands everything."

"Yes, sir," Mr. Stubbs said respectfully. "To be sure,
an occasion such as this will need some special fitting out,
particularly if the gentleman has just arrived from India.
Just the other day, we fitted up a dozen gentlemen from
the Dark Continent who came straight from the aerodrome. They arrived here barefoot and they left half an
hour later turned out like our gentlemen. In the olden
days, I used to fit out many of the officers going across
the seas to carve out the British Empire from the bush
and the jungle."

"I must, then, have seen your handiwork often," Delinquent Chacha said. "You know, I was brought up
nearly exclusively in English company. Perhaps you
turned out our good Deputy Commissioner. Mr. Stubbs,
if the cut of his suit or the quality of his brandy was ever
admired, he was such a gentleman that he lightly passed

over the compliment and gave the credit entirely to his tailor or wine merchant. He used to say you can tell a good, aristocratic shop by the size and extent of the credit it allows. When he was at Ox-Ford, apparently any undergraduate could go through the University without having a penny in his pockets. The bills simply waited until the young man found his feet—got established in society, you know—or his inheritance fell due."

"Not quite anymore, sir," Mr. Stubbs said sombrely. "Some of the riffraff going up to the University nowadays come from such backgrounds that they have never seen a fiver in their lives. A few of us in London, however, still try to keep up the old tradition. But a bad debt *is* a bad debt, and even we cannot hold off the arm of the law."

"Yes, yes," Delinquent Chacha said abstractedly. "Shall we commence?"

"I expect you would like to pick up some shirts first," Mr. Stubbs said.

Delinquent Chacha spent the morning in the shop. He ordered six pink silk shirts, but he objected to the plastic buttons and insisted on mother-of-pearl instead. After the shirts, he selected a pair of gold cufflinks, to be engraved with the initials "D.C." He chose a broad mortarboard with a red tassel, a long crimson gown with white facing, a dozen fire-cracker-red ties and matching socks, a pair of brown fleece-lined boots, and an assortment of suède shoes. He also had himself measured for a couple of pairs of breeches and for half a dozen purplish-blue suits, in a fitting room that, to his great delight, was lined with mirrors, saddles, and whips. Once, I whispered in his ear "How will you manage to pay for all this?" but he brushed me aside. He made dates for the fittings with Mr. Stubbs and we walked out of the shop without further mention of money. On the corner of Oxford and Regent Streets, Delinquent Chacha closed his eyes and said, "O Ram, even though I have been canonized by the Christians, it is you I thank."

A MONTH later, I went down to meet Delinquent Chacha at the Oxford station. At first, I did not recognize him. He got off the last car of the train and was standing next to three enormous suitcases. He had on the mortarboard, with the red tassel dropping down over his right ear, and the long crimson gown with white facing reached nearly to his ankles. Under the gown he was wearing one of the pink silk shirts and one of the purplish-blue suits. He looked more like a fairyland vice-chancellor than my uncle.

"Oh, Kaka!" he said when I went up to him. "Your Delinquent Chacha feels like the Rajah of the United Nations." Following my glance to the suitcases, he said shyly, "My trousseau—or most of it. I had to part temporarily with one or two suits to get some ready cash from Lala Suraj Pal."

Delinquent Chacha nodded to the ticket collector and a porter, who seized the luggage. Arm in arm, Delinquent Chacha and I walked out of the station. The porter packed the luggage into the boot and the front seat of a taxi, and Delinquent Chacha acknowledged his bow with a ten-shilling note and a wide sweep of the hand. Delinquent Chacha had some trouble in arranging himself, since his clothes took up nearly half of the seat, and we set out for my college, on High Street, where I had booked him a guest room for the weekend. During the long, dull drive toward the center of Oxford, Delinquent Chacha said, "I have the peroration and the body of the lecture firmly in mind—I have spent every waking hour since I received the invitation working on them—but the introduction still escapes me."

As we were passing the theatre that was to house the General Assembly, I pointed it out to him. "Hold the engine!" he shouted to the driver, and sat looking at the rococo building long and hard. "Let's have a dress rehearsal," he said thoughtfully. "It's best to subdue the stage of one's début from the start." We jumped down, but the theatre turned out to be locked. "Tallyho! Away to your college," he said, and we set out once again. The introduction—or, rather, the lack of it—kept us up all that night. He refused to budge from his seat on my big sofa in front of the fire, even to change into his comfortable pajamas, though after some discussion he did put his mortarboard aside. In the hope of charming the Muse, he toasted his hands by the fire, drank large cups of coffee, smoked cigarettes. So that his concentration might be complete, he even made me his amanuensis, but no sooner had I written down a sentence like "All the eggs of the human race are now in one wicker basket" than he would ask me to cross it out and start again. By breakfast time, we had nothing to show for the labor of the night except heavy eyes and flushed faces.

We were having a feast of kippers in the college hall when he looked up from his plate and said, "I've got it. It's come to me, Kaka! The portraits of the hallowed sages which line these walls, sages who have inspired countless generations of undergraduates, have done their work on me, too. Oh, those wise old birds! My opening is going to—" He put down his knife and fork and looked around for an audience. Except for a few early risers eating their breakfast in forbidding silence behind newspapers, the hall was discouragingly empty. "Perhaps I should preserve the freshness of my introduction by not saying it. Words when repeated sometimes have the look of a rose sat upon."

THE platform was decorated with the colors of more than a hundred countries. More flags waved high up on either side of the auditorium. Young and eager faces, mostly English, were everywhere. A couple of workmen in overalls rushed around, adjusting a camera near the back wall, testing microphones at the ends of the rows, aligning cables, and hammering nails into flagpoles. Some students gesticulated and talked as though they were prima donnas and their words and expressions were being caught even at that moment by the cameras and tape recorders.

Two young men—one short and squat, with a beard and a patched-up tweed jacket, one tall and angular, with long hair and thick glasses—slouched on the steps of the stage. They seemed to be in charge. Delinquent Chacha marched up to them, and I tagged along. He stood patiently waiting to be noticed, but the two continued to study the seating charts for the delegates, the observers, and the press. Delinquent Chacha cleared his throat several times, and when they still failed to notice him he announced in a clear, ringing voice, "Delinquent Chacha, C.M.G., here!" The two young men started and looked around. The one with the beard introduced himself; he was the President of the General Assembly. The tall boy with the thick glasses was the Secretary-General. Delinquent Chacha was escorted onto the stage and presented to the other speakers, who were seated somewhat inconspicuously on a long bench at the back

65

of the stage, and I found a seat in the stalls. In comparison with Delinquent Chacha, the other guests looked shabby and insignificant. The best-dressed of them, an African in tribal dress—apparently Chief Lulu—gave Delinquent Chacha a deferential smile and moved over a little on the bench. Delinquent Chacha sat down. From where I was, he appeared a little lost, though the crimson of his exotic gown gained, if anything, from the setting.

The fall of the gavel opened the meeting. After some fiery words of welcome by the youthful Secretary-General, the President introduced the first speaker: "Alas, I am but little acquainted with this marvellous man in gorgeous livery, but clearly he is a rising star in the industrial India of tomorrow."

In a voice that filled every corner of the hall, Delinquent Chacha said, "Mr. President . . . Mr. Secretary-General . . ." I saw that he was standing dangerously close to the edge of the platform. "My fellow-speakers . . ." he continued. "Ladies and gentlemen . . . I give you Delinquent Chacha, the Companion of the Order of St. Michael and St. George!" The audience dissolved in laughter, with Delinquent Chacha joining in. He waited benignly for the last ripple to die down before resuming the speech. "I have had my fun and games. Now I only wish to serve Her Majesty as an effective citizen of this great and good world. Alas, because of the temptations of poker parties, procreation, and general love of constant company, I neglected the things of the mind and

66

frittered away my youth. I am just forty-seven. Indeed, I was that proverbial swine who, as a piglet, was unable to see the pearls cast before him. But now, with your kind indulgence, I should like to change all that before it is too late. I beseech you to make me a new man in a hurry by the golden force of legislation, that cornerstone of the just and nearly lasting dominion of the British Empire, so that my picture, too, may hang in the hall of an Ox-Ford college and one day inspire the lambs coming up to the fountain of wisdom."

There was a general confused whispering in the auditorium. Undaunted, Delinquent Chacha went on to recite the clauses of a resolution, which he promised to have copied and distributed before the end of the plenary session: "Whereas in India the bulk of wheat and curry food and the hot, torpid weather—not to mention the temptation of gossip, juicy as a mango—sap away all desire to edify the mind; whereas in accursed India there is not, nor ever has been, the tradition of the printed word; whereas in hallowed England there is the champagne climate, the tradition of learning and ready stimulus of professorial minds cunningly grouped together in a few historic universities; whereas Delinquent Chacha is no longer a whippersnapper but a veteran, a mature man; whereas at last Delinquent Chacha has the opportunity to read to his heart's content in the light of the gentle wisdom all around him and to benefit therefrom; whereas his life's ambition has been to become a member of an Ox-Ford common room; whereas he has a burning wish to save the world—therefore, we, the members of the Ox-Ford Commonwealth Polytechnical College, the Cowley Secretarial Bureau, the Ox-Ford Parktown Crammer for Young Ladies, recommend that at least one principal of an Ox-Ford college give Delinquent Chacha an opportunity to attend this hallowed institution." He finished the text of the resolution to an explosion of happy applause.

"As I look down," he resumed, "upon your young faces—shining cheek of a youth here, demure downcast eye of a damsel there, the Marxist-red goatee of the President beside me, and the dappled, dignified head of the Secretary-General on my right—I can't but shake in my boots with emotion for the life of all mankind. The cobalt bomb threatens to bring down the rosy world of our dreams around our ears. It is not for nothing that the sage Einstein, who was as privy to the mysteries of the universe as the great Lord Krishna of old, declared once, 'I don't know about the Third World War, but the Fourth will be fought with stones.' Stones of the irreplaceable Chinese Wall, stones of the Acropolis, stones of the Hagia Sophia, stones of the Russian steppes, stones of Niagara Falls, stones of the Grand Canyon—stones of our beloved and sacred and bewitching Taj Mahal."

A prolonged and persistent hiss, at first barely audible and then almost as loud as Delinquent Chacha's cathedral voice, developed in the loudspeaker. It became a gheelike voice. "Point of personal information, Mr. President. It has precedence, does it not, over all points except points of order?" The voice belonged to a slight, spidery man with a long, thin face, dark as a charred tree. He danced around a floor microphone, ominously swinging the gooseneck.

The President said, "I recognize the honorable chairman of the delegation from Pakistan, but I should be grateful if he would be brief."

"The chairman of the Pakistani delegation will be very brief," the gheelike voice went on, "if his point of personal information is satisfied." There were murmurs of impatience in the hall. "In his turn, the chairman of the Pakistani delegation would be grateful if he could be assured that his ears have not deceived him—that is to say, his hearing has not become suddenly and inexplicably defective. For I have every reason to believe that as little as ten minutes ago—nay, five—my ears were clean as a police whistle and worked no worse, no better—"

"I am bound to repeat that I should be grateful if the honorable chairman of the Pakistani delegation would be brief," the President broke in hesitantly.

"Did I hear," the oily voice continued, unaffected by the rebuke, "the honorable speaker from India describe himself with a *handle* to his name?" There was laughter in the hall. "Did I hear the honorable speaker from India say he was C.M.G., a handle which, I am led to believe from my reading—perhaps not as diligent or attentive as it might have been—is furnished only by the English monarch to Englishmen serving in the hardships of foreign embassies and foreign parts?"

"You did," the President said.

"Thank you," the chairman of the Pakistani delegation said, and abruptly sat down.

There was a burst of laughter from the hall, and some uncertain applause. The President informed the chamber that it would be difficult for him to countenance any more interruptions from the house. At a signal from him, Delinquent Chacha continued with his speech. In a voice at once mellifluous and majestic, he described what he called "the rosiest dream of my country"—the Taj Mahal. "Here, ladies and gentlemen, is a building of milk-white marble, and here the terraces, gardens, turfs, and still waters. Here, ladies and gentlemen, are the domes, rising like marble bubbles into an azure sky, and here the columns, glistening with agates, bloodstones, and jaspers. Here there are rows upon rows of flowering shrubs, commemorating life, there the countless dark cypresses commemorating death and eternity. The sheer, limpid, frozen beauty of this sweet dream in marble alters by the hour of the day, even as Lord Krishna changed his incarnations—it is cold and gray in the dew of the dawn, a shimmering white in the blaze of noon, a tender rose in the lingering afterglow. At all hours, it is a veritable white cloud, hanging in the vault of the sky."

With his hand beckoning feverishly, he took a few steps back. "Will the members of the United Nations come inside and perch awhile on the former site of the Peacock Throne, or will they instead kneel at the cenotaph of Emperor Shah Jahan and his queen, Mumtaz Mahall, whose glories the memorial enshrines for eternity? Hush that vulgar sound!" he suddenly shouted at a hint of a hiss in the loudspeaker. "The cenotaph responds to such noises only as a sounding drum. Sing, rather, the seventh chord and listen to the bewitching results!" Delinquent Chacha sang out something approaching the notes of the seventh chord. "Do you hear the chord, my people? Listen." He cocked his head. "It is caught up in the echoes of the roof; it reverberates in endless harmonies. It sends up sounds like angelic hymns issuing from the throats of a celestial choir; it haunts the air above and around and comes down in distilled showers upon the polished marble. It rises, falls like the stuff of dreams. Oh, ladies and gentlemen, think not that the Taj belongs only to India. It belongs to you."

Delinquent Chacha went on to tell how masons from Baghdad, dome builders from Turkey and Samarkand, mosaic workers from Kanauj, calligraphers from Shiraz, flower carvers from Mongolia, and inlayers from Florence had given substance to Shah Jahan's dream; jade and crystal had flowed in from China, turquoise from Tibet, lapis lazuli from Ceylon, coral from Arabia, diamonds from Bundelkhand, onyx and amethyst from

Persia. Was there a man in the hall who could say that in his heart he did not know the great, sweet dream? "Is not its message that of inspired love?" Delinquent Chacha thundered. "Love of man for woman, love of nation for nation, love of peace, harmony, and happiness? I declare to you that every man carries the Taj Mahal in his breast pocket—nay, on his cheek. As the hallowed sage has pronounced, the Taj Mahal is no less than 'a teardrop of love on the cheek of time.' "

Suddenly the hiss developed again in the microphone. It was once more the delegate from Pakistan. "Mr. President, point of order this time!"

"I recognize the chairman of the delegation from Pakistan on a point of order," the President said shortly, to murmurs of strong disapproval in the audience.

"The chairman of the Pakistani delegation wishes to be enlightened if parliamentary-procedure rules permit him to request the most honorable speaker from India to yield the floor."

More like a trades-union leader than a viceroy, the President scratched his head and said that in all honesty he did not know. He invited comments from the floor on the procedure at issue, and this resulted in a heated and inconclusive debate. Delinquent Chacha helpfully declared from his bench seat that he would hear what the good gentleman from Pakistan had to say.

The Pakistani chairman thanked Delinquent Chacha, a little sarcastically, and sailed into a long speech of his own. Was the honorable gentleman from India aware that the Taj Mahal was perhaps the most sacred, the most cherished monument of Muslims from the Indian Ocean to the Red Sea, from the Persian Gulf to the Atlantic Ocean? Was he aware that the Taj Mahal, the crown of palaces, wonder of wonders, was a shrine of perhaps the greatest Muslim king for his queen, snatched from him by an early tragic death? Was he aware that the cenotaph to this day carried an inscription commemorating the most beautiful Mogul queen? If so, how did he have the cheek to defile the memory of the Mogul empress by calling the monument Indian? Indeed, the Pakistani delegation had already drafted a resolution which would force the Indian government to give back the holy place to its rightful and true owners and arrange for safe access to it through a special corridor.

"Zionists say, 'What are a people without their land?' " the Pakistani chairman went on. "But I ask you: What are a people without their history, without their holy monument? The love of land, the acquisition of property are bourgeois concepts." There were boos from the audience. "But the Taj Mahal is a different matter. For us," the Pakistani added wistfully, caressingly, "the Taj Mahal is second only to Mecca."

At least a dozen delegates were on their feet, shouting for right of reply. The worried President recognized the chairman of the United Kingdom delegation.

"I should like to remind the Assembly," the English-

73

man said calmly, "that the city of Agra, where the Taj Mahal is situated, is some hundreds of miles from the nearest Pakistani city of Lahore."

"What of that? You slide rule! Calculate the distance between West and East Pakistan, West Germany and Berlin!" a girl cried out.

The President called for order.

"I am aware," the Englishman went on, unruffled, "that the two lobes of this newly born country of Pakistan are spaced far apart. But at least they are two enormous, economically self-sufficient units. The Taj, on the other hand, is no more than a building, and, short of taking it brick by brick to Pakistan and rebuilding it, my country had no choice but to let the mausoleum— for that is what it really is—remain in India. Any reasonable man will see that the decision was sane, unavoidable, logically sound. . . ."

While the Englishman was speaking, the members of the Pakistani delegation rudely left their seats and drifted into the aisle to whisper. The spidery chairman, detaching himself from the huddle, now interrupted the United Kingdom's defense. "Point of order, Mr. President!" Without being recognized, he went on. "O Allah, Allah, wicked are the ways of the Kaffirs. My suspicions, the direst of them, have just been confirmed by my delegates."

The President asked the honorable gentleman from

Pakistan to either address himself to a "point," if he had one, or sit down.

"So be it, Allah. Point of order. I'm afraid, Mr. President, I have the onerous duty of pointing out to you that we have allowed all this while a veritable cobra to nestle in our bosom." There was a confused murmuring on the floor, and whispering and stomping of feet from the galleries. "Yes, a cobra!" the Pakistani went on emphatically. "No political question can be settled, however small—let alone the biggest of them all, the question of the ownership of the Taj Mahal—until we seize this serpent, squash its head, and pluck it out."

The President nervously ruled that the harsh remarks of his Pakistani friend were out of order.

"They are anything but, Mr. President," the Pakistani said. "Wait till I tell you who this serpent is. He has such a beguiling mask for his lethal fangs that he's all the more poisonous, all the more menacing. Ladies and gentlemen, I ask you to search your hearts, and if you are that serpent, step forward so that we can resume the work of this Assembly by the cleansing effect of a public confession. What, Allah, no one comes forward? Then be it on your head, Chacha! This clown," he went on, wagging his forefinger fiercely at Delinquent Chacha, "masquerading as a man with a handle to his name, ludicrously appearing in the livery of a vice-chancellor, was formerly one of the more renowned good-for-nothing

75

loafers in Multan—as it happens, the home town of one of my delegates. And even though now it is in Pakistan and he has departed, his pre-partition notoriety lives on. I am told that he is now connected with a restaurant near Shaftesbury Avenue, where, ladies and gentlemen, he is to be seen opening the doors of taxis!"

IN the safety of the train to London, all the unnerving happenings of the morning—the failure of the President to give a satisfactory explanation of how Delinquent Chacha had come to be invited, the fistfight between the Indian and Pakistani delegations, the flying inkpots, the blinding flash bulbs of the photographers, the muscular Indian who ran out of the Assembly Hall with Delinquent Chacha on his back and snatched the mortarboard as a relic—seemed no more real than any nightmare, and Delinquent Chacha, never one to look back, least of all on bad dreams, quickly recovered his spirits.

The next day, there was an account in the newspapers of the Model United Nations row at Oxford, and the School and University Outfitters of London started a legal action against Delinquent Chacha. I learned of this by accident. I was putting off going to bed by glancing through the haphazard pile of newspapers and magazines allowed to accumulate on the large table in the middle of the Junior Common Room and had arrived at the editorial page of the *Observer:* yet another piece by the Master of an Oxford college, proposing yet another way to modernize Oxford and bring it into line with the twentieth century; conditions in British prisons; extending hospitality to West Indians; and one final item, with the heading "Argument from Excess." As I read the first sentence, the paper almost dropped from my hands. "On the surface, a porter of an Indian restaurant in Soho, earning his keep and seventeen-and-six a week, is not a piece of news, certainly not a comment on Britain in the sixties. But this is, in fact, the case. 'Delinquent Chacha,' as the porter calls himself, is a highly civilized, intelligent, and keen Indian who has a nephew at Oxford, and who, if it were not for the wounds of the British raj, with its false emphasis on class superiority and form for form's sake, might today be an exemplary citizen of his country—indeed, any country. As it is, he must stand trial for what Inspector Jones of Scotland Yard calls 'allegedly dressing above his station and going around with a handle to his name.' The porter apparently obtains credit easily by passing himself off as a titled gentleman. In fact, as such, he has been up to Oxford to speak. Surely the fact that an employee of such a restaurant should have outstanding tailors' bills upward of five hundred pounds, and should feel the need to dress in

Regent Street clothes at all—which are but the facts—
says something about present-day Britain. Actually, in a
sense, it is not so much an indictment of him as of
ourselves. We have national health care. We are groping
toward an equitable national system of education. Some
of our most forward-looking intellectuals are already
talking about nationalizing property. Is there not an
argument for checking the excesses of affluence and the
extravagance of taste and dress that they encourage?
One might reasonably ask whom are the lords and ladies
with their titles and high Edwardian lapels and minks
trying to impress? No one is arguing for uniformity of
dress and taste; the argument from excess should not be
confused with that. It is simply questioning whether
expensive and outmoded trimmings make any sense in
the Britain of the sixties." I was left numbed.

The next morning, I found a large manila envelope
lying on the floor outside my oak. It was addressed to
me in Delinquent Chacha's hand; the curlicues and
flourishes were unmistakable. Inside was a sheet torn
from a pad of telegram blanks, as though Delinquent
Chacha had intended to send me a wire. After carefully
filling out my name and address and the previous day's
date at the top of the blank, and noting it was afternoon,
he had written:

KAKA NO TIME FOR STYLISTIC FINERIES STOP YOU SEE
OBSERVER HEARTENING EDITORIAL ON ME STOP DELIN-
QUENT CHACHAS WORK INTELLECT FINALLY ACKNOWL-

EDGED BY ENGLISH PEOPLE STOP THEIR OPINION ALONE
COUNTS STOP ONE WORD IN OBSERVER BETTER THAN
HUNDRED IN TIMES OF INDIA OR NEW YORK TIMES STOP
HARK EXCLAMATION CALLED AROUND OBSERVER TO CON-
GRATULATE THEM AND DOWNED HALF A PINT OF BITTER
WITH ASSISTANT EDITOR AT NEARBY PUB CHARMINGLY
CALLED OLD AUNTIE STOP HE HAD GOOD SUGGESTION TO
TAKE OUT ADVERTISEMENT IN NEW STATESMAN AND ASK
FOR CONTRIBUTIONS TO DELINQUENT CHACHA FUND FOR
DEFENSE AND PROCURING SOME AMENITIES OF LIFE FOR
ME STOP SAYS THING OFTEN DONE FOR STARVING WRITERS
ARTISTS WITH SUCCESS STOP WOULD LIKE TO ARGUE
CASE MYSELF STOP AM PUZZLED STOP ANY VIEWS QUES-
TION MUST SIGN OFF STOP OH COMMA NO WORD OF TRIAL
SHOULD REACH EARS OF FAMILY FOR THEIR BASIC LACK
OF KNOWLEDGE OF WORLD WILL LEAD TO UNNECESSARY
WORRY STOP FONDLY CHACHA.

On the back of the sheet there was a bit of hasty
scribbling in his normal hand: "Written with a bursting
heart. Oh, that your Delinquent Chacha were so well-
heeled that this important communiqué could be
urgently dispatched by means of Morse Code—da-dá,
da-dá."

Optimistic though the letter was, the fact remained
that he *had* helped himself to suits, shirts, neckties, and
other accessories at the shop of School and University
Outfitters without letting on that he was penniless.
What defense under the circumstances he hoped to put
up for himself I could not imagine. The tailor charged
him with fraudulently obtaining clothes and credit, and

79

he was obliged to appear at a preliminary hearing in the magistrate's court, where he was remanded for trial on a criminal indictment. He engaged to defend him a barrister named McLean, who was a client of the restaurant. As Delinquent Chacha waited for his case to come up, such comfort as I could give him was limited to writing letters. Neither of us could spare the money for Oxford-London trunk calls.

THE case was tried in an almost empty courtroom. The judge, the counsel for the defense, Mr. McLean, the prosecutor for the Crown, Mr. Munlop, instructing solicitors, and a jury of three spinsters with feathers on their heads and nine men in flannels, two with bowler hats and spectacles, all seemed to blend and at times disappear into the stark, formal architecture of the room.

"Contrary to Section 32 (1) of the Larceny Act of 1916," the court clerk droned, "the particulars of the offense being that you, between the twenty-eighth day of December, 19—, and the fourth day of January, 19—, in the city of London, with intent to defraud, obtained from the School and University Outfitters (London), Ltd., coats, trousers, waistcoats, shirts, neckties, studs, shoes, stockings, garters, a gown, a mortarboard, and other accessories and apparel to the value of five hundred and seventy-eight pounds, three shillings, and two-pence by falsely pretending that you were a Companion of the Order of St. Michael and St. George." He turned to Delinquent Chacha in the dock. "How say you to this charge—guilty or not guilty?"

"Not guilty," Delinquent Chacha replied. Standing at ease, his head slightly tilted, he listened attentively.

"You are further charged with the offense of obtaining credit, contrary to Section 13(1) of the Debtors Act of 1869, the particulars of the offense being that you, between the twenty-eighth day of December, 19—, and the fourth day of January, 19—, in the city of London, in incurring a debt or liability to the school and University Outfitters (London), Ltd., obtained credit to the amount of five hundred and seventy-eight pounds, three shillings, and twopence from the said School and University Outfitters (London), Ltd., under false pretenses or by means of fraud *other* than false pretenses. How say you to *this* charge—guilty or not guilty?"

Again Delinquent Chacha said, "Not guilty."

The judge gave a little cough and, chin in hand, leaned toward the counsel for the prosecution, who, scarcely glancing at the papers before him, launched into his opening statement: "Members of the jury, it may seem to you that since the accused is a foreigner, he should not be expected to know the subtleties and the symbols of our culture; say, to realize the distinction between 'C.M.G.' and 'E-s-q'—one the prerogative of Her

Majesty the Queen to bestow, the other the prerogative of a gentleman, which nowadays, I think it would be generally acknowledged, does not amount to as much as it once did, though that is not necessarily to say that abuse of either designation is to be countenanced. In other words, it may seem to you that a foreigner, in his ignorance, might think we use 'E-s-q' and 'C.M.G.' interchangeably."

"Your Lordship." It was Delinquent Chacha's voice, soft but firm, addressing the judge. There was a stir in the courtroom. The counsels for the prosecution and the defense looked severely at each other; the court clerk half stood up; the members of the jury looked at Delinquent Chacha and then at the judge.

"Do you wish to say something?" the judge asked.

"Your Lordship," Delinquent Chacha continued, "just now a grave aspersion has been cast on my nationality and general knowledge. At heart I am an Englishman, and *ipso facto*"—he bore down on the Latin words as though to impress upon the court that he was not unacquainted with the vocabulary of the law—"not a foreigner in any sense of the word. It is in India that I am an alien. I am acquainted not only with the distinction between E-s-q and C.M.G. but with K.B.E., O.B.E., K.C.S.I., O.M., K.O.S.B., K.G., O.St. J.—"

"My Lord," the prosecuting counsel broke in, "I really must protest this interruption. I was in the middle of my opening statement."

82

"We are aware of that," the judge said, but his curiosity seemed to have been aroused. Turning back to Delinquent Chacha, he asked, "Are you, then, a British citizen?"

"British subject, Your Lordship. It comes to the same thing. India is still a member of the Commonwealth."

"I see. And do I understand you to say that you do understand about titles of honor?"

"Your Lordship, very much so," Delinquent Chacha said.

A look of horror crossed the face of the counsel for the defense. The court clerk took off his spectacles and put them on again.

"This is most serious," the judge said, frowning. "You admit, then, that you knowingly appropriated to yourself a title the bestowal of which, as counsel for the prosecution has put it, is one of the prerogatives of Her Majesty?"

"Your Lordship, Your Lordship!" Delinquent Chacha cried out. "Who said I appropriated to myself a title? I was persuaded that Her Majesty had given me one."

"Given you one?"

"Yes, Your Lordship. It was a case of genuine misunderstanding between her and me—my wish becoming a horse, if you see what I mean."

"I'm afraid I do see," said the judge.

The defense counsel rose, but the judge was making notes and did not look up. The defense counsel waited patiently, his gown thrown back, his hands behind him.

"My Lord," he said, when he had received permission to speak. "My learned friend Mr. Munlop was good enough, in the course of his opening remarks, to refer to the possibility that my client might, in all good faith, have failed to appreciate the distinction between C.M.G. and E-s-q. I can only express my real indebtedness to my learned friend for having so nobly espoused the cause of my client"—he paused for laughter in the courtroom—"even if I know from past experience that my learned friend is kind only to be cruel later." More laughter. "But then my learned friend should not take umbrage if our *joint* client feels constrained, in the circumstances, to rise in defense of his honor and his intelligence."

He sat down, and the counsel for the prosecution now went on with his opening statement: "Members of the jury, as I was about to say before I was interrupted, it has been suggested by a so-called independent news-paper—which you may have read prior to coming here and to which I must refer in order that I may clear your minds—that a great leap of imagination is required in this case if the gap between the Orient and the Occident is to be bridged. It has been implied that colonialism is nothing but the rule of one class over another, the sway of upper-class rule over the proletariat of the world, and that when the solid barriers between classes, between rulers and ruled, collapse—as, it is al-leged, they have done in our time—people, in their insecurity, will fasten on anything whereby they can perpetuate the old system, particularly if that system works in their favor. The gravamen of this argument is that it is doubtful whether an underprivileged man can be blamed for giving himself the airs and pretensions of a man of privilege, especially if he doesn't realize the consequences. Happily, such grandiose sentiments, using a particular case or man as a scapegoat for one's sociological predispositions, are not the ways of the law. I entreat you, first of all, to purge your minds of all this claptrap. And, second, if my learned friend Mr. McLean should go on to argue that the accused has a vivid fantasy life, I would ask the members of the jury to ask themselves which of us does not, and whether a vivid fantasy life, short of proved insanity, gives one the right to cause injury to others. Thirdly, should an attempt be made to shift the guilt of the defendant to society at large, I would ask the members of the jury to remember that the charges in question have to be settled, if there is to be law at all, on narrow legal grounds—in this instance, as set forth by the Larceny Act of 1916." He read from a paper in front of him the relevant sections, and then continued, "Should my learned friend Mr. McLean see fit to argue that the accused had *intended* to pay one day, then I would beg the members of the jury to remind themselves about the *facts* of the case, which, taken together, leave no doubt that the motive of the accused was nothing other than to obtain these goods by deception and to dispose of them afterward. Or why else would he order and buy, as he did, six identical suits, six identical shirts, a dozen identical ties and socks—not to question the use a man of his humble station might have for an academic gown and a mortarboard, which he also bought."

"Your Lordship!" Delinquent Chacha called out. "I bought the cap and gown to go up to Ox-Ford. I still hope to be a student there in the Ruskin Delegacy for Adult Education."

"The point is made," the judge said, and waved to the prosecuting counsel to continue.

"*Mutatis mutandis*, the same kind of argument applies to his assortment of shoes and boots and breeches—with extra watch pockets, if you please. Needless to say, the defendant wears a wristwatch."

Delinquent Chacha held up his hand and exhibited his large Mickey Mouse watch.

"You see the gall of the man!" the prosecutor thundered, not realizing that Delinquent Chacha was trying to be helpful. I felt like speaking out in his defense, but I told myself, as I did many times that day, that I was a helpless spectator, with no choice but to sit and listen and hope. "Nor is that the limit," the counsel for the prosecution was saying. "Do you see that bizarre suit, that pink shirt, that red tie, those red socks, those suède shoes that the accused has on? They are all the clothes in question, the property of the complainant, all bought on

86

credit extended to the accused as a direct consequence of his false and cunning pretenses."

Turning to Delinquent Chacha, the judge asked, "Prisoner, is it true, what has just been alleged?"

"Of course, Your Lordship," Delinquent Chacha said. "I have no other clothes to my name. And let me say that in all my life I've never had clothes which fitted me better."

The judge then asked the court clerk if the prisoner had pleaded guilty to either of the charges—one of false pretenses, and the other of incurring debt or liability, obtaining credit, and fraud. The court clerk answered no, and the judge indicated that the prosecuting counsel was to go on.

"And what about the complainant, the complainant whose business depends on good faith and extension of credit? He is out of pocket *five hundred and seventy-eight pounds, three shillings, and twopence!* You may well whistle under your breath, ladies and gentlemen, for the complainant cannot recover this staggering sum even if all the accused's emoluments, which are seventeen-and-six a week, *seventeen-and-six,* are attached for years—nay, aeons. And what do you make of the following? Clothes not paid for—mind you, clothes probably *never* to be paid for—were sold to a third party, one Lala Suraj Pal, the employer of the accused. This is not the end of the collusive transaction. Actual *cash* was exchanged between the accused and this third

87

party, with, need I add, not so much as a farthing sent in the direction of the complainant. There are, I submit, only three simple questions at stake here. *Did* the accused, as charged, under this and other false pretenses, obtain from the complainant the apparel and accessories in question? Even disregarding the intentions of the accused, did he then, as charged, obtain the apparel and accessories without means or hope of paying for them? Did he later part with some of these garments to realize cash and profit? If the answers to these questions be in the affirmative—and can you have any doubts?—then you should have no hesitation in declaring the accused guilty and putting him behind bars, where he belongs. My Lord, shall I proceed to call my witnesses?"

Half a dozen exasperating exchanges about technicalities then followed. The prosecuting counsel wanted to call up Lala Suraj Pal first, but as a hostile witness, on the ground that he had disavowed his original deposition to the police. In the end, the judge agreed to this.

Lala Suraj Pal, looking massive and prosperous as ever in funereal black, waddled into the courtroom and heaved himself into the witness box. In spite of the prosecuting counsel's volley of leading questions, Lala Suraj Pal kept to the new version of his story, which was that though he had never before lent money, the thirty pounds he had given to Delinquent Chacha was not for clothes but was a loan; that he had accepted the clothes only as security for the loan; that, in any case, he could have no possible use for the clothes, since Delinquent Chacha's girth and shoulders were twenty-six and thirty-four, respectively, while his were forty-four and fifty-two. He had said in his deposition to the detectives that he *had* purchased the clothes because he was frightened by any policeman. Lala Suraj Pal talked haltingly and with effort. His lined forehead was wet with perspiration.

"I suggest to you," the prosecuting counsel said, "that at the back of your mind you knew all the time that you could pawn your share of the loot and get back twice or three times the money you lent your servant. In giving him thirty pounds and accepting clothes valued at a hundred and thirty pounds, eleven shillings, you were at best acting the part of a usurer. You have disowned the deposition and changed your story now because of the collusive transaction. *Is that not the truth?*"

"Your Lordship!" Delinquent Chacha called out. "My heart bleeds for the dire predicament of my dear employer, who has given me a place to rest my head ever since I arrived in Britannia."

The prosecuting counsel opened his mouth to object, but sat down when Delinquent Chacha said, "Could my master hold that both versions of his statement are true?"

"I'm not sure I follow your meaning," the judge said.

"My learned friend Mr. Munlop"—the prosecuting counsel winced—"and Mr. McLean both might be found to fully contradict each other and yet be telling the truth. From my conversations with the Lala previous to my indictment and arraignment, I can assure you that he does not believe in lies any more than I do, but only in degrees of truth. I'm now talking, of course, as a philosopher; I have had a bent toward the subject all my life, as my nephew will testify, if you will call him to the witness box." He turned around and called to me, "Kaka, come!"

"My Lord," the prosecuting counsel said in a voice as loud as it was furious, "if the excesses of the defendant are not curtailed—"

"Mr. Munlop," the judge said wearily, "my sympathies are entirely with you. Because of the accused's unfamiliarity with the procedures of a court of law, I have allowed him considerable latitude. But I agree—this is too much!" He then sternly admonished Delinquent Chacha to cease his interruptions and to permit his own counsel to present his case in due course.

"May I, then, not summon my Kaka?" Delinquent Chacha asked.

"Let the prisoner be advised that no defense witness can be called until the prosecuting counsel has rested his case," the judge said.

The examination of Lala Suraj Pal now continued. "Which is true, the deposition to the police or its denial?" the prosecuting counsel asked.

"Just as my servant says, both my stories are true," Lala Suraj Pal declared.

The judge asked for the remark to be repeated several

times. He then patiently enumerated the contradictions between the two versions of Lala Suraj Pal's story and said, "Before you give your final answer, I want to draw your attention to the fact that in this country perjury is a very serious offense. You may already have perjured yourself, but in view of your unfamiliarity with our laws—"

"Your Lordship, the Lala has lived in this country for thirty years, and he's a real English-fashion gentleman, not a native wallah at all," Delinquent Chacha cried out.

"Would the defense counsel see to it that we are not interrupted?" the judge said severely. Then, to Lala Suraj Pal, "This is a matter of delicacy. In view of your unfamiliarity, then, I would like to give you another chance to tell the truth. Do not be afraid of us. We are not the police."

But in spite of this and subsequent warnings of perjury from the judge, for the remainder of the prosecution's examination Lala Suraj Pal could be prevailed upon to say nothing but "It is all true."

"My Lord," the prosecuting counsel finished, turning Lala Suraj Pal over to the defense for cross-examination, "in my time at the bar I have never had a more exasperating witness than the present one."

"Lala Suraj Pal, would you tell the court under what circumstances you made the acquaintance of the accused?" Mr. McLean then asked.

Lala Suraj Pal suddenly became expansive. "Acquaintance? How can that be difficult? These days, business in the Indian restaurants is none too good, especially for the honest ones. The more unscrupulous of them are serving kitty-cat and beef. Others have called in the aid of dancing girls and you-know-whats. As Ram is my witness, we have been advertising on our door the temple-like purity and silence to be found within, the exclusive use of mutton, and the absence of all fleshly temptations except the God-given one of nourishment and sustenance. But where, O Ram, is such honest advertisement to take root in these foul times, when holy cows are bred only to be slaughtered? The Bhagavad-Gita says, 'Do your duty, and the reward is in the laps of the gods,' but—"

"My Lord, I fail to see the relevance of this commercial for the All-India Taj Mahal Curry, Chutney, and Soup Restaurant," the prosecuting counsel broke in. Despite the interruption, the defense counsel sat down, yielding the floor. "Nor am I able to see what possible relevance the defense's probing of the meeting of the witness and the accused has to do with the charges at hand."

Instantly the defense counsel was on his feet. "One of the main elements of the case presented by the prosecution is that a man in the position of Delinquent Chacha, a porter at a restaurant, could have no other reason for acquiring these clothes than to resell them at a profit.

The defense will show, however, that the character and outlook of the accused are such that it is perfectly natural—indeed, inevitable—that he should have aspired to the clothes with no other motive than personal use. To establish this, evidence must be presented bearing on the life and habits of the accused, and, short of procuring witnesses from India to this end, no one is in a better position to provide this than the Lala, who has been acquainted with the accused since the day he arrived in England, three months ago."

"Hear, hear! Good show, McLean!" Delinquent Chacha called out, and was admonished from the bench.

The prosecuting counsel withdrew his objection, and the defense counsel's cross-examination continued. "Though the accused is, in England, a porter earning seventeen-and-six a week, in his own country he's a man of consequence, who might well afford handsome clothes from a shop such as School and University—"

"How can he afford?" Lala Suraj Pal said petulantly. "His karma is to be a poor relation for life. It is the dharma of his family, who are blessed with the good things of life, to see that he does not walk about in the street naked and hungry, or they will have a price to pay in the next birth. It is their duty to water and nurse the weak plants of their household, and Delinquent Chacha has enough wisdom to see they do, for poor relations are placed by the gods to remind the rich and successful that the world is maya."

That disposed of the defense's contention that in his own country Delinquent Chacha could aspire to expensive clothes. "Cross-examination finished," the defense counsel said, and the Lala stepped down from the stand and ambled out of the courtroom.

The next witness was the clock winder from the Royal Colonial Club of the British Empire. After being sworn in, he stood in the box with cap in hand.

"Did the accused often come to the club?" Munlop asked.

"Often."

"What did he do?"

"Just passed the time of day admiring the building and the ties—we have regimental and club ties in a showcase in the hall—but, most of all, writing out his name, with the title, in the visitors' book."

The visitors' book of the club was produced as an exhibit by the prosecution and examined by the jury. A specimen of Delinquent Chacha's signature was then requested and obtained. The members of the jury scrutinized it, the three spinster members asking to see the book again.

"The book is filled with it," the clock winder was saying. " 'What's the necessity?' I asks the gentleman. 'What's the harm of it, Jimmy?' he says."

"Did you believe that the defendant had been topped by the Queen?" Munlop asked.

"It was not for me to question."

94

"Did you ever press him on why he signed the visitors' book so often?"

"He said it himself. 'I tell you, Jimmy,' he says once, 'I have thirteen children—' "

"Which is the truth, Your Lordship," Delinquent Chacha broke in.

" 'They're all farmed out to my successful brothers,' he says, 'for good keeping and education, you know— and no doubt a few grandchildren are going to be on the way soon. That kind of thing goes fast in my country, and I should like my granddaughters and grandsons to have a record of their grandfather's having whiled away his time in a club as grand and hallowed as this. I am not the first gentleman in the world without a fortune, but I make up for it with good connections and constant vigilance to cultivate the great figures of this world.' "

"Jimmy, you've talked a lot," Mr. McLean said during the cross-examination, "and I frankly don't know to what purpose." The prosecuting counsel stood up and then sat down. "But I want you to think about this question. Think about it hard. Did the prisoner ever do any harm by signing his name in your visitors' book?"

"I'd never have allowed him in the club. That's harm plenty."

"But did he do any harm?"

"No, can't say he did."

"My Lord, that's all from the defense."

Inspector Jones was the next witness. He related the

circumstances of Delinquent Chacha's arrest at the restaurant.

"Did the accused say anything when you charged him with an offense and gave him due warning not to say anything incriminating?" the prosecuting counsel asked.

"Yes, sir. He said, 'I always knew something like this would happen.' He seemed to be worried that his family in India had put the police after him. It seems he stole away from home."

"Your Lordship, that I did," Delinquent Chacha called out, "or I would have been prevented from leaving home altogether."

With a sigh, the judge addressed Delinquent Chacha once again. "You really must not interrupt in this manner. There are limits to my forbearance, and I must warn you that my patience is wearing thin."

Delinquent Chacha, however, thanked him graciously.

"Then what did he say?" the prosecuting counsel inquired.

"Well, sir," Inspector Jones said, "when I told him I hadn't come on behalf of his family he instantly set up a wail. At first, I couldn't make out why he was carrying on like this, but I gather that he thought I'd been sent by Her Majesty to take away his title."

The judge looked puzzled. "Do you mean to say that at the time you served the summons upon him he really thought that a title had been conferred upon him by the Queen?"

"My Lord, all I can say is that as soon as I informed him that I was not from the Queen he plied me with questions about whether the Queen could ever withdraw honors once conferred and, if not, whether there was any forgotten historical precedent for her ever having done so. When I was able to get in a word, I explained that I was ignorant of the working of the honors system and that I was there simply because of a complaint laid by the School and University Outfitters, Ltd. He then asked me whether these proceedings could cause the Queen to withdraw the honor, or, if the honor had not as yet been conferred—and this was the most confusing part—whether the proceedings would effectively prevent such an honor being conferred one day, which leads me to believe that maybe he knew all along he was not entitled to the honor but was nevertheless hoping for it to be conferred someday in the future."

"What happened when you finally got the charges through to the accused, or, rather, got him to focus on them?"

"Well, he became very interested, and he said, 'England as I've come to know it was too good to last.'"

"What did he mean by that? Did he explain?"

"Well, not exactly, but he said that the shop he was dealing with was really fifth-rate. 'Now, Inspector Jones,' he said, 'what do you think of a tailor who holds the measuring tape not close to his stomach but an arm's length from his body? Tailors who really know how to

97

wait on gentlemen hold their tape . . .' At this point, I stopped taking down his words, since they didn't seem to me particularly relevant."

"What happened after that?"

"He tried to press some tea on me."

"Did you accept?"

"No, sir. I was on duty. I would not on duty. But the accused had a cup. He got very friendly. 'My dear Inspector Jones,' he said, 'I would like to have you as my friend. If I had my choice, we would be thick as thieves.' Those were his exact words, sir."

" 'Thick as thieves'?" the prosecuting counsel repeated significantly.

"Yes, sir, but I don't know what he meant by it. I don't know if it was just misuse of the language or whether he wanted me to become his partner in crime."

"What did you think?"

"To tell the truth, sir, I couldn't make heads or tails of anything the accused said."

"Thank you," the prosecuting counsel said. "My Lord, I have finished."

The defense counsel had no questions.

Mr. Stubbs was called to the witness stand. After two or three preliminary questions, he was asked to describe what happened the day Delinquent Chacha came into the shop.

"Well, sir, we talked a bit about the subcontinent. I used to fit out many of the gentlemen going out there in the old days. And then his nephew joined us and the gentleman set about selecting his wardrobe." Mr. Stubbs went on to give prices and produce bills as exhibits for each of Delinquent Chacha's purchases. "He mostly liked gabardines, worsteds, and silks," Mr. Stubbs continued, "and his color preferences ran to pinks, reds, purples, and blues. In fact, sir, the gentleman has on some of the clothes he bought that day."

"The gentleman has *on* some of the clothes he bought that day," the prosecuting counsel repeated, and paused meaningfully. "Thank you, Mr. Stubbs. The defense may proceed with the cross-examination of the witness."

"The clothes which the prisoner selected," Mr. Mc-Lean began, "how did you feel about them?"

"Feel about them? At first, I did think it was a little peculiar that the defendant should want so many clothes and of such colors, but then I have served enough maharajahs and men from the tropics to know that they do go in for identical clothes and eye-aching colors—eye-aching from our standpoint. Perhaps not so eye-aching, sir, when you think about the uniforms of our schools and universities."

"And did you ever think of denying the prisoner credit?"

"No, sir. For one thing, it was a rush order; the gentleman had a speech to make. But, in any case, ninety per cent of our business is done on account. We supply uniforms to boys in scores of schools. Our customers

start with us when they're at Eton or Harrow or Win-
chester and stay with us through the rest of their lives.
We have made clothes for Guardsmen, peers of the
realm, and foreign royalty, and it would never do—it
would be impractical, sir—for us to make trouble about
opening accounts. The gentleman did say he hoped to go
up to Oxford. Purple and blue could have been the
colors of his college."

Now came Delinquent Chacha's longest interruption.
It seemed to be in the form of a story. "Your Lordship,"
he began, raising his voice so that it would carry
throughout the courtroom, "I had a premonition of
some disaster overtaking me sooner or later—"

The prosecuting counsel rose to his feet and said, "My
Lord—"

The judge shrugged, and settled lower in his chair.

"All the while," Delinquent Chacha continued, "I had
kept my eyes open for a Q.C. As you know, the business
at the restaurant is none too good. In fact, if we get nine
customers a day we count ourselves lucky, and though
lately we have been advertising on the door how quiet it
is—not a small thing in this noisy metropolis—it has not
had much effect on our commerce as yet, or, rather, it is
too early to tell. In any case, it's not very difficult to
strike up an acquaintance with such stragglers as do
grace our portals, and not long ago a gentleman walked
in whose bearing was such that I knew right away he
was not an ordinary man. I showed him to a table and

said, 'What will it be, sir, today? Shrimp in house chutney sauce—' It's my usual drill. He chose sparingly and
ate like a bird—a sure sign of good breeding here in
England. He was a little diffident at first, but I brought
him out, you know. I learned that he was of Scottish
extraction, and a barrister. Apparently, for the first ten
years these barristers get very little work, since they still
have their name to make. I think, though, he will make
his mark sooner than most, since he has already the
appearance and the manner of a razzle-dazzle. Throughout his first visit, I pressed on him repeated invitations to
come and dine at the restaurant. When he didn't come
again for a whole week, I thought he must have met with
a fatality. I was debating calling on him on my first free
afternoon, ready to drink to his health if he were well,
offer sorrowful condolences if he weren't, when School
and University Outfitters laid their complaint against
me. I had an added incentive for looking up the razzle-
dazzle. I took a bus up to Fleet Street and walked around
to the Strand entrance of the Temple. The visit couldn't
have opened more propitiously. As soon as I came within
earshot of the Temple gates, what should greet me but
the sound of a marvellous drum roll and a military bugle.
I soon saw the reason for it. A drill of a cavalry regiment
on the Temple grounds was in progress, complete with
horses and white-coated sweepers with shovels in hand
to clean up after the horses. Your Lordship, it was that
kind of discipline and organized approach to life that

was the stuff of the British raj. At first, because of the din, I didn't quite get the directions of the porter, who, incidentally, is called Bitte, and, taking a wrong turn into a staircase, ended up in a coal cellar. But another smoke and consultation with Bitte and, like a fox, I arrived at the door. I gave a few raps with the knocker. That started a chain of circumstances which, though at first light as a feather on my wrists, have now grown heavier than the heaviest shackles. Your Lordship, my meaning is I was persuaded to let McLean—for that is who the gentleman was—take on the case when he offered to do it for nothing. He said, 'The pennies you could ever send my way wouldn't buy one log for my fire.' I've been in this court now for many hours, and things have been going from bad to worse. I feel that McLean has let me down, not lived up to my expectations of a razzle-dazzle, so am I at liberty to relieve him of his burdensome duties and argue my own case? McLean, my dear fellow, no hard feelings—"

"My Lord"—it was the prosecuting counsel—"the strategy of the accused is quite clear. It is to compound the confusion and escape. He has turned the whole proceedings into some form of Oriental melodrama, and now he says to his own counsel, 'Do not darken my door.' If the legal profession in Britain is to maintain its dignity—"

McLean, who had been talking earnestly with his instructing solicitor, now rose and addressed the court.

"My Lord," he began, "we are faced with a most unusual situation. My client has expressed in open court his lack of confidence in my ability to present his case effectively and has sought your permission to discharge me of my duties. I am an officer of the court and, as such, responsible to the court for the manner in which I represent my client. The precedents, such as they are, appear to indicate that you have a discretion to accept or reject the request made by my client. It has been stated on the one hand—here I refer to R. v. Woodward (1944) K.B. 118— that once counsel has begun to conduct the defense and has cross-examined witnesses, the prisoner cannot be permitted to dispense with the services of counsel and conduct his own defense. On the other hand, it has equally been decided—and here I refer to the case of O'Brian who shot Sir Henry Wilson and de Courey— that a person charged with a criminal offense cannot have counsel forced on him against his will. My Lord, I accordingly find myself in a difficult and embarrassing position. Your Lordship will already have noted—perhaps with a certain degree of apprehension—that the accused in this trial has displayed what may be described as a disregard for the limitations imposed upon him by the need to have defense counsel present the case on his behalf. Your Lordship may, accordingly, wish to take into consideration the fact that if with your permission I were to withdraw, the accused would then be enabled to do what he so obviously wishes to do—namely, to conduct his own defense in the manner he thinks best suited to the circumstances. I should be greatly indebted to Your Lordship if you were to see fit to relieve me of a burden which I find increasingly difficult to discharge both to my own satisfaction and to that of my client." McLean resumed his seat.

The judge, glancing at the clock above the entrance to the court, remarked, "Thank you, Mr. McLean. I see that it is nearly time for the court to adjourn. I propose to take the accused's request into consideration, bearing in mind the points so forcefully urged by Mr. McLean, and give my ruling in the morning."

The judge adjourned the court. Delinquent Chacha was led out by two policemen through the passage under the dock.

THE following day, I returned to the court, after a sleepless night in a nearby bed-and-breakfast place. When the judge convened the court, McLean was there.

"I now propose," the judge began, referring to his notes before him, "to give my ruling on the request of the accused yesterday afternoon for permission to dispense with the services of his counsel. I have not failed to observe that the conduct of the accused has not been consonant with that relationship of trust and confidence which should exist between client and counsel. And yet I have not felt constrained to interpret the accused's repeated outbursts as implying disrespect for the court. Had I done so, I would have visited upon him the sanctions with which I am empowered. In according a considerable degree of latitude to the accused, I have also been influenced by the fact that the accused is obviously unfamiliar with the workings of the machinery of justice in this country. If I have granted to the accused a greater degree of liberty than I would normally have accorded, we have to remember that he is standing trial in an alien environment—it is said that in the East impulse has greater dominion than reason—and that, as the old saw has it, justice must not only be done, it must also be *seen* to be done."

Here the judge coughed, consulted his notes, frowned, and then resumed, "However, not once did I envisage that my indulgence of the accused's outbursts would fill the accused with such confidence in his own powers of advocacy as would make him imagine he could take on the burden of representing himself here. I must interpose at this juncture that the eagerness of the accused to conduct his own defense is not, to my knowledge, fortified by any particular training in the intricacies of the law. Howsoever this may be, I cannot ignore the plea which has been made to me by counsel for the defense, Mr.

McLean, to permit him to withdraw from the case. Bearing in mind the principles established in O'Brian who shot Sir Henry Wilson and de Courey, I propose, in the exercise of my discretion, to grant this permission. In so doing, let me make it quite clear that I do not for a moment accept the allegation of the accused that counsel for the defense has been remiss in his duty either to the court or to his client. On the contrary, I wish to express my admiration and respect for the manner in which he has conducted himself in difficult circumstances."

The judge now turned to address Delinquent Chacha. "The accused will understand that I am, in effect, acceding to his request to take over the conduct of his own defense. I have some misgivings about this, but, as custom requires, I intend to give the prisoner such assistance as I may properly accord to him. And I would request you, members of the jury, to bear in mind that the accused will be laboring under some disadvantage, and that your duty is not to judge the accused by his demeanor in this courtroom but, instead, to render a verdict—yea or nay—on the evidence laid before you."

"Hear, hear! Well spoken, Your Lordship! Let the trial proceed!" Delinquent Chacha called out.

"And now," said the judge, ignoring him, "we were in the middle of the cross-examination of Mr. Stubbs. The accused is at liberty to address questions—relevant questions—to the witness."

At this point, Mr. McLean rose, gathered his robes

around him, collected his various papers, bowed to the judge, and swept out of the courtroom. Mr. Stubbs was called for, and, after being warned that he was still under oath, presented for cross-examination.

"Let us suppose," Delinquent Chacha said, in his best legal manner, "that a member of the jury or His Lordship wanted to have an adornment to his skin such as I have on at present. How would he go about it? And as for that adornment, I should like to submit the following exhibit." Delinquent Chacha turned around and held up his coattail. "Does everyone in the court see how this seam is coming undone?"

"He would come in and ask for an account, sir," Stubbs said hastily.

"He would, of course, have to give you references," the judge broke in.

"For our records, Your Lordship, we would ask for the name of his bank and at least a couple of other shops where he might have accounts."

"We would like to hear what references the accused gave."

"Your Lordship," Delinquent Chacha broke in, "I didn't give *any* references to the School and University Outfitters."

"Well, in the beginning, before the gentleman's nephew arrived, Your Lordship, I *did* ask the accused for references, but the question somehow got lost in the flow of conversation. I can't remember now, but I could have assumed that the gentleman had an account with us, since I don't remember ever having got a direct answer to my question about references. We often don't know which of our gentlemen have accounts with us and which of them don't. Unless they tell us to the contrary, we assume they do. If the gentleman says, 'Put that on account,' we automatically assume that he has an account."

"Did the accused, then, say, 'Put that on account'?"

"More than once."

"And your accounts department, didn't it tell you that there was no such account?"

"They can't, until the clothes are made. We don't make up the bills until then."

"One would have supposed that that was bad business."

"We find it advisable, Your Lordship, not to make up the final bills until the clothes are made. Sometimes there are extra charges for alterations, and we have no way of knowing the charge until we have made the alterations. Sometimes the pattern the client selected has been discontinued, and we have to ask him to come in and select another. It may differ in price. Sometimes the pattern is out of stock—the pattern the gentleman selected for his suiting *was* an old one—and the makers reissue it later at another price. Sometimes the customer isn't satisfied with the clothes and wishes to return them; we like him to feel easy in his mind about doing so. Your Lordship, we have been tailors two hundred years, and we have a tradition to keep up."

"Your Lordship," Delinquent Chacha said, "all you have to do is to walk into old Stubbs' shop and say, 'I am So-and-So,' select as many suitings as you like, and say, 'Thank you, put that on account.' It's as easy as a shoehorn."

"Is that true, witness?" the judge asked, leaning forward on the table.

"If someone says 'Put that on account,' Your Lordship," Stubbs replied, "we assume he has an account, unless he looks suspicious. Everyone will grant, Your Lordship, that the accused looks like a gentleman."

"Do you mean to tell the court that the fact that I was a mere commoner or C.M.G. or had a barony or an earldom wouldn't make any difference to you?"

"Not for opening an account, Your Lordship."

"Do we understand that you would open one automatically for anyone who walked in from the street and did not look suspicious?"

"Yes, Your Lordship."

"Bless me!" the judge exclaimed. "Are you telling us that the whole question of the false pretenses, the burden of the first charge against the accused, is an irrelevant one? If anyone can get an account at your shop, it would appear that the fact that the accused passed himself off as a Companion of the Order of St. Michael and St. George didn't influence you for better or worse."

"And now, Stubbs," Delinquent Chacha said, when he was permitted to examine the witness, "you will not object if I ask you a few more questions? Good. I should like to know—and I am sure His Lordship would be equally interested to hear—how long, on an average, you permit an account to remain unpaid before you take your honored client to court?"

"Anywhere from a month to three years. On the average, nine or ten months."

At this point, the judge addressed the witness: "And what was the period of time between the accused's purchase of these garments and the date when your firm laid an information against him?"

"About a month from the date when he first ordered them, and two weeks from the date when the clothes were delivered to him. But, Your Lordship, it was only then that we realized that we were dealing with a man of straw. . . ."

SHORTLY thereafter, the judge began his summation. "On the one hand, members of the jury," he declared, "there can be no law unless guilty men are punished. On the other hand, men may leave us in no doubt of their guilt—indeed, flaunt it—yet unless they can be proved guilty under the law, they cannot be punished if there is to be any law. Keeping this in mind, what, then, can we infer from the witnesses produced against the accused? The testimony of Lala Suraj Pal, the first witness you heard, is less than worthless as far as the charges against the accused are concerned, and I have no choice but to advise you to strike it out of your minds as you set about your weighty task of determining, under law, the guilt or innocence of the accused. For that witness's testimony, because of its flagrant contradictions, might prove *him* guilty of perjury, but that guilt cannot be allowed to cast a shadow on the accused. And, as for Inspector Jones, he simply succeeded in communicating to us the confusion he himself felt, without irrevocably establishing harm done to anyone. The testimony of the clock winder of the Royal Colonial Club of the British Empire does not leave us with any room for doubt that the accused does in fact use the title of Companion of the Order of St. Michael and St. George, but here again, unless the use of the title by the accused in the presence of Mr. Stubbs induced the latter to hand over the goods to the former without immediate payment—and Mr. Stubbs' testimony goes against our supposing this—the use of the title cannot be held to be germane to the case. Therefore, you should acquit the accused on the first charge. The second charge is more difficult. It is now my duty to instruct you that, to convict on this charge, you must be satisfied that three elements have been proved: one, that there has been an incurring of a debt or liability; two, that there has been an obtaining of credit; and, three, that there has been fraud. You may well feel that there is little doubt as to the first two elements. But you must be equally satisfied that fraud has been proved. In this connection, you will wish to consider as a whole what evidence exists as to the intention or ability of the accused to pay this outstanding account. I would draw your attention to the fact that the complaint was laid by the School and University Outfitters, Ltd., barely two weeks after the clothes had been delivered to the accused. You are entitled here to draw on your own experience to determine whether this lapse of time, combined with the other factors in the case, sufficiently indicated the intent of the accused *not* to pay. You may also consider it significant that the date when the complaint was lodged coincided with the date of certain press reports concerning the extraordinary activities of the accused at Oxford. These reports, as you will recall, revealed for the first time that the accused was not, as he had claimed to be, entitled to the style and designation of a Companion of one of our orders of chivalry. As to the *ability* to pay, you will, of course, bear in mind that the outstanding account is for a very large sum and that the accused occupies a humble and not very well-paid position. As

against this, we know very little of his family back-
ground in India, and it could be that, like a certain
famous character in fiction, he was confidently, although
perhaps over-optimistically, waiting for 'something to
turn up' which would enable him to meet his commit-
ments. These, members of the jury, are matters for you
to determine. I cannot assist you further, but would
merely beseech you, before you retire, to bear in mind
that you must determine these matters on the evidence
which has been laid before you in this court, and on no
other basis. In particular, you should not be influenced
by any prejudice for or against the accused based upon
your opinion of his personality, conduct, or temperament, which may appear to you peculiar and puzzling or
exotic and engaging, depending on your own personality,
conduct, and temperament. And now I leave these issues
in your hands, confident that you will render a true and
fair verdict according to the evidence."

ASTONISHINGLY, the end of the day found Delinquent Chacha a free man, back at the All-India Taj Mahal Curry, Chutney, and Soup Restaurant. Inside the restaurant, over large cups of Ceylon tea, he dictated to me, rapidly, a letter to Queen Elizabeth II of Britain:

"My dear, dear Your Royal Highness: I salute you with the two fingers of my left hand on my forehead and with a low bow from the waist. Even though our paths have never quite crossed, I venture to write to you in this direct and urgent way because of the great peril facing your Empire. From my cursory perusal of the lessons of history, it seems to me that two qualities built the British Empire and kept it sunny side up with its best foot forward: carefully framed legislation, and show of authority. Of the two, authority is the more important, for without it legislation is impotent. For the purposes of authority, your royal and august ancestors worked out a careful system of bewitching gradations and hallowed honors for services rendered, and such was the justness and power of these gradations that every grade of honor was automatically given its due homage by the people of the world.

"It is to this issue that I now wish to address myself. Not long ago, I was at Oxford, attending a meeting of the Model United Nations, and I witnessed a scene that in its pandemonium can only be compared to the Sepoy Mutiny. It strengthened my conviction that if Britain is to continue as a great power and be an island of order in this topsy-turvy hurly-burly of a world, such rebellions have to be quelled. I offer my services. I beseech you to make me a Knight of the Order of the Garter (C.M.G. is not enough) in a hurry, so that I can help you ride out the storm. I shall be glad to call upon you any time in order to receive the rap of the chivalrous sword on my shoulder. Meantime, perhaps you would be kind enough to forward the application for my coat of arms to the appropriate heraldic college. I would like the dispenser of seals to keep in mind my three hobbies: cards, love of the people, and addiction to coffee and eating places. Perhaps my seal could show a friendly cuckoo looking at an ace of spades and holding a few Brazilian coffee beans in its claws.

"Believe me, etc.

"Chacha."

Nothing I said could dissuade him from posting the petition.

Format by Lydia Link
Set in Linotype Janson
Composed, printed and bound by American Book-Stratford Press, Inc.
HARPER & ROW, PUBLISHERS, INCORPORATED